Advance Praise for
A Rhapsody for the Eternal

"Darren Speegle is a remarkable new writer."
—Lucius Shepard, author of *Softspoken*

"Elegant, sometimes intense and horrific but always finely crafted and devious in the best way, these stories will delight and entertain fans of dark fantasy."
—Jeff Vandermeer, author of *Shriek: An Afterword*

"... one of the most intriguing voices active in genre fiction."—*Cemetery Dance*

"Darren Speegle is a real discovery."— Graham Joyce, author of *The Exchange*

"...Speegle's voice and worldview are bizarre and mesmerizing, humane and compelling, and the stories contained in this collection will fry your mind. Bleeding between horror, dark fantasy, science fiction, as well as all things heartbreaking and nerve-wracking, Speegle's stories could best be described—if it's possible to describe them at all, and I'm not sure they should be—as "the savage cerebral," something you've not encountered much before. That's because Speegle doesn't write fast enough. You'll agree with that last statement before you're halfway through this exceptional collection."
—5-time Bram Stoker Award-winner Gary A. Braunbeck, author of *Coffin County* and *Far Dark Fields*

"Darren Speegle's characters, and their situations—in his often brilliant stories— are brought vibrantly, horrifically to life, because he cares about his characters, the stories he tells through them, and the words he chooses, with such great care, to bring them to the printed page. He's among the best writers I've read; sitting down with his new collection, *Rhapsody*, was a real joy for me both as a reader, and as a writer."
—T.M. Wright, author of *Blue Canoe* and *Bone Soup*

Other Books by Darren Speegle

Gothic Wine
A Dirge for the Temporal

A Rhapsody for the Eternal

A Short Story Collection

by Darren Speegle

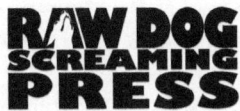

Published by Raw Dog Screaming Press

Hyattsville, MD

First Paperback Edition

"The Lunatic Miss Teak" previously published in *Subterranean: Tales of Dark Fantasy*, 2008

"Elephant Speak" previously published in *Postscripts*, 2007

"The Man in Window Three" previously published by Scrybe Press, 2005

"Transtexting Pose" previously published in *Clarkesworld*, 2007

"Glitzing with the Big Delicious" previously published in *Fortean Bureau*, 2005

"Night Watch" previously published in *Phantom*, 2006

"A Last Word" previously published in *SpecFicWorld*, 2004

Cover image: Steven Archer

Book design: Jennifer Barnes

Printed in the United States of America

ISBN: 978-1-933293-77-6

Library of Congress Control Number: 2009925974

www.RawDogScreaming.com

How I long to throw myself into endless space and float above the awful abyss—Goethe.

For Julian, my best Scot and friend

Table of Contents

Let thy strings ring frantic
Beneath the bow
Thy fabric bleed molten
Thy stitches enthroe

I know thee well
Tapestry of mine
Enthralling, thy babel
Ensnarling, thy twine

The Lunatic Miss Teak

If I'd foreglimpsed any inkling of what was in store for me that evening, I'd have turned back as soon as I rounded the crook in the valley to behold Castle Cochem perched there upon its strategic hill above the River Mosel. As it was, what foreboding did pay a visit came from the fortress itself. Splendidly menacing, its many pointed turrets contrasted a coral, dusking sky that seemed to reflect the vast fresco I knew adorned the opposite wall of the castle's main structure. This was the same feeling I'd experienced when I saw the Schloss for the first time. Indeed, why had I come back to Cochem, Germany, ten years later, except to know that sensation again?

The feeling that immediately followed the sense of impending woe—again, just like a decade before—is harder to describe. It is an artist's feeling, a touch of something greater than we are. Even a word as encompassing as "inspirational" falls short. To one who plies his trade by his sensitivities, the foreboding itself could be said to be inspirational. It is as misleading a term as it is incomplete. No, what is delivered by an experience like Castle Cochem is more of the quality of the divine, a glimpse into the nature of existence. It's nothing to do with history or architecture or civilization in general. It's to do with our relationship with ourselves, with nature, the universe, God. Am I a conduit? No. A mirror? Yes. Accurate or distorted, reflection is my game. And that's why I had come again, to reveal the thing that had haunted me, like so many other things have haunted me, through the years.

At the hotel they greeted me with knowledge. Maybe my agent Francis had written ahead, maybe Love, the latest protégé Francis had dug up in her continual pursuit of keeping up my image—whatever that meant. In any case they knew me at the Hotel Weinheim as a commercially successful—perish the term—painter from America. After quickly setting them straight, I was walking the cobblestone streets of Cochem again as a friendless nobody, a wayward unheard philosopher, just the way I liked it.

The avenues unrolled before me, lamp lit passageways of the soul's maze, each pool of light a false promise, an illusory moment in the most ephemeral thing of all: life. I was in that sort of temper, see. Where the past is gone and the future hasn't happened yet and only the moment exists? It is the place I both retreat and aspire to, the one certainty, the one reality other than the existential pain itself. The moment. It is the crux of all philosophies, the nexus of all roads. It is what it is, no more or less. It speaks to the vast futility of existence without losing itself in its words. For words, too, are gone, as surely as they haven't happened yet. As certainly, as absolutely as that.

For a thousand cents she can be yours.

I stopped, staring at the sign in the window; shivering in the summer air. While I had passed windows brimming with the samples of watch vendors and doll dealers, traders of the curious and exotic, exploiters of the moment, my receptors had been in pause mode. Now they were alive, a Descartesesque testament to my own reality. For a protracted instant in time, as I stood there captured by the message, I understood what it all meant. God. That's who the words referred to. She could be mine for a thousand cents. Ten euro. She was a whore and I was her john, and all the rest of it, dressing. Like one of my paintings, her image appeared spontaneously, saturated the cavities of my mind. Warmly curvaceous, suggestively sinuous, stinking of the floral, earthy, carnal fragrances of Eden. Then my eyes fell to the object the sign referred to and the moment was gone, leaving only a sticky film that was usually accompanied by a cigarette or a trip to the toilet to piss away what's been done in order to make room for the now. My eyes fell to the object and I transformed back into the ignorant fool trying to say something to the world and having nothing to say. Particularly at this moment, with the vault emptying of its voluptuous outlines, its dirty musks, its insane hope for something more, even something so seedy and debasing as a *bought* fuck from God.

She was a puppet, or mannequin, or something representative. She was jointed, freakish, and ugly, and apparently made of teak, as was indicated by the sticker pasted over her left nipple. *Miss Teak*, it read in all its subtlety. Beyond the doll's grotesqueness, beyond its pointless existence except as an artistic work—and who knows, perhaps at another moment I would have appreciated it for that—what stood out about it were the numerous inch-long horizontal slots that covered its torso, occasionally revealing light from behind its evidently similarly pocked back. Maybe it was to do with the limbs appearing so dully solid as they rested at bizarre angles to the body. It sat, did this doll thing, in some limp and broken imitation of powwow style, yet there was a lust for life about it that was only partially attributable to its twisted, toothy grin. In that regard I suppose I did see it as an artistic representation, though I didn't register any effect beyond the shock of its appearance, the fiercely disorganized, un-German-like nature of it even as it was being presented to English speaking tourists. That and my inexplicable desire to own the thing, to have it in my nonexistent collection of weird global souvenirs. So strong was this desire that I actually experienced a profound relief when I found the shop door open. At eleven pm, this was an amazing discovery, but I didn't care about such superfluities at the moment. My focus was in one direction and would not be satisfied until the doll hung over my shoulder, chuckling obscenities into my shirt as it escorted me back to the hotel room.

For a thousand cents…

The lady behind the counter possessed a grin to rival the lunatic Miss Teak's, though it wasn't nearly so offsetting in its human guise. She greeted me with the usual "*Abend*," but that's where all pretenses toward normalcy ended.

"She is a steal, yes, at a thousand cents? Have you brought found coins or are you interested in company of a lesser sort?"

"Excuse me?"

"Miss Teak. You can be hers or she can be yours. It is a decision yours to make."

I didn't know what to say to her; no level of improvisation would suffice. So: "Ten euro, right?"

"A thousand cents is the price, yes. Euro, dollars, it does not matter. But you are not a tourist, are you? To linger so long over her? I think she knows you."

I stepped to the window, picked up the doll. She rattled, wood on wood. A clear teak song in the dense hollow between words. The shopkeeper's dark, knowing ones, my aimless, uncertain ones as I walked to the counter, mumbling, "Your English is impeccable, ma'am."

"I think you know her, too."

I pulled the money out of my wallet. The temperature was too high in here. I could feel sweat somewhere. Skin and fabric. The delicate probe of the shopkeeper's eyes. The soft chuckle of Miss Teak, burrowing in, making herself available to me. *You can be hers or she can be yours.*

The ten euro note stuck to my hand. I had the image of teeth and pulp. Dribbling juice. An empty branch in a full garden. *It is a decision yours to make.*

"Does she have a first name?" I heard myself say as the bill came unattached from my skin.

"But you already know the answer to that, I think."

"Eve?" I said. "Is it Eve?"

"Look at her. Was Eve not created in God's image? A thousand cents, sir, and you can be hers as well. Found coins. Don't go looking for them. Find them where they present themselves. On the street, in the gutter, in a forgotten pocket. This is the only way. Happenstance is what life is all about, is it not? Protein molecules. Lightning. Shop windows. Let the coins find you and you can be hers. If that is what you want."

"Is that what she wants?" It wasn't my own mouth; they weren't my own words.

"But I think you know the answer to that question, too." Her widening grin was a savage extension of itself. "I hope to see you again, sir. Before the sun sets on the flock. Before the rivers and the moon have turned to blood."

Before the rivers and the moon had turned to blood. That hour was approaching the moment fast.

II

When I returned to my home in Hartford, Connecticut, I found a surprise waiting for me. First, as I entered the house with my travel bag in one hand and Miss Teak in the other, my cat Jayjay greeted me with a vicious hiss, hackles rising like brethren in arms before she fled to some unknown location. My first impression was that she didn't like Miss Teak. Then I saw the feathers.

They were everywhere, from one end of the house to the other. As I went from room to room, I discovered that her no doubt terrified playmate had shat on the walls, the couch, the kitchen counters. Wherever the bird had found temporary haven, it had soiled what was beneath it. Jayjay had done a number on the poor creature, and God only knew what shape its remains were in. I knew from experience that Jayjay left only the entrails of mice and rats that she brought in through the crack I always left in the sliding glass door. This time I didn't know what to expect. Do birds even have entrails to speak of, or do they have a grit-oiled processor in there to take care of the ingested matter? Was I going to find an intricate machine about the size of a walnut? I hoped so, because entrails are not fun even on their best days. It's not the gore that gets you so much as those small blood-tainted pools of saliva or bodily fluid—take your pick—found off to the side. At any rate the frenzied trail eventually led me to the plant room, where, lo and behold, the bird roosted on one of the branches, alive and in urgent condition, with a broken wing and no tail feathers whatsoever remaining.

I donned a pair of garden gloves and while in the process of catching the poor creature and letting it gently out the window to be devoured by some other carnivore, recorded strange noises from Jayjay in the hall. I watched the bird manage to hobble its way across the lawn to the cover of the shrubbery, then stepped out of the room to assess the next situation. What I found sent a nasty thrill through me. My cat was arched poetically before Miss Teak where I had dropped her, hackles rising so high now, she looked like she was on fire. The thrill in my veins surged to my head as Jayjay more than proved my first impression correct. Normally docile, she appeared on the verge of striking the invader in our home. No sooner had I conceived the thought, *Get away from her, Jayjay*, than Jayjay was flung backwards into the wall.

I stared wonderingly as she flipped back onto her feet again and shot off down the hall, literally sliding across the hardwood as she rounded the corner. My God, I thought, Miss Teak is one of those magical curiosities you read about in stories. But I knew that to be a misplaced assessment even as I was placing it. *I* was the culprit. Miss Teak was a part of it, I'd no doubt, but my own will had tossed the cat into the wall. The knowledge of power suddenly bloomed in me, consuming the wonder, the shock, the fear that was, quite frankly, unbecoming of my magnificence. I stared at the door of the plant room and it slammed shut at my bidding. Beside it the wall ruptured then fell into place again, showering plaster on the floor. I called the dust to me and it came, dancing in a miniature whirlwind in front of my face. I was a song to the world. The lives I would save. The hungry bellies I would fill. The diseases I would cure. The wars I would—

My eyes landed on the coin. It lay there against the molding, just beside Miss Teak, whose grin seemed to be focused in that direction. The power high faded as quickly as it had come, and I knew what I must do. At my will the coin rose into the air, spun there a moment, then dropped into one of the slots in Miss Teak's body. For an instant in time the glass eyes of the doll shone, but that too might have been my will.

"What shall we do with you then?" I said to Miss Teak. But my thoughts were on numbers. One down and nine hundred ninety-nine to go. Then I would be hers, whatever that meant in the scheme of things.

"What are you, Miss Teak? The devil? God?"

The only reply was a distorted grin accompanied by a long undulating whine from whatever niche Jayjay cowered in.

~

I was mine now. Why would I want to be hers? But I learned the answer to that soon enough. Without her proximity I could not use my power. And even with her present, it proved to have its limitations. Case in point: the harmless outcome of my first descent into road rage after I'd come into Miss Teak's company. The car cut in front of me, barely missing my bumper, and I willed its rear window to explode into a million pieces. Though Miss Teak sat in the backseat smiling her crazy smile (I liked to have her with me there at the beginning), the window did not obey and the asshole driver went on about his reckless way. I spent the whole of three seconds wondering what had gone wrong, and then it came to me. Danger. Not as applied to the driver, but as applied to me. Blatant displays were forbidden. Attention would be drawn. The equilibrium of things would be set awry. The earth's axis would tilt a degree and across the Atlantic some British yeoman in full beefeater array would betray his post, losing his straight face at the taunts of tourists. If I wanted to play with my power, I must do so in private. Limited miracles of the healing sort were okay, as I learned during my first post-acquisition trip through a hospital. They could be attributed, however wrongly so. They could find a home in someone's heart. Blatant displays could not.

It was a strange balance, and one I'd no choice but to come to terms with. This I did by stepping aside, or forfeiting resistance wherever the force sought to flourish. Oddly, the one area where it manifest itself most plainly was not in its capacity as an employable tool, but in my art. My conceptualizations assumed deeper meaning as the blurry lines that separated the supposed or hoped for from what I can only describe as aesthetic truth sharpened to a razor edge fineness. Unbidden, undreamt of images surfaced, images that would pass along their existential impact by speaking directly to the psyche of the finished work's beholder. The first paintings to come out of this fugue swept the industry with a seemingly internal, predetermined momentum. My previous body of competent yet improvable work disappeared into oblivion as my collaborations with Miss Teak led to soaring acclaim. My work was described as glorious and decadent, exalting and intensely disturbing. Inevitably, in becoming this icon I lost touch with the common people, formerly my bread and butter. Such adjectives as exalting and disturbing do not complement each other well among the working glass. Sales of prints faltered, while my originals fetched exorbitant prices at shows that essentially became social parties for the bloated. Eventually Francis convinced me to get out of the print market entirely. After that I became like certain artists before me. Alone. Alone with my work and the finite power behind it.

I might have surrendered to madness like certain artists before me as well had I not retained a necessary measure of context and self. Whenever my descent would approach its oblivious nadir, perspective shone back at me out of the darkness like Miss Teak's eyes at the taste of a coin. I had the potential means to accomplish greater things, to change humankind, not just offer glimpses into its condition through my art. Had I not already committed myself to that end? If confirmation was needed, if the light flickered in the abyss, I would hoist myself up out of my slime and go look at the holes that had steadily been disappearing from Miss Teak's torso as she kept physical count of every coin I'd dropped since bringing her home with me.

III

It took years, but finally only a single slot remained. The one thousandth. I was deep into the mud of my solitude by then, a vastly wealthy hermit artist who could no longer be bothered to attend his own shows. In spite of this I could not bring myself to pick up that last cent, though every time I emerged from my cave it seemed there was one waiting for me by a curb or under a kicked rock. In time I quit going out altogether. I could not endure the sight of lost or discarded coins. I could not endure the thought of becoming hers even as I so desired that very thing.

Then the dreams began. Vivid and savagely real affairs that filled the voids between paintings. The first one affected me most profoundly, I think, because it brought Miss Teak to life in a way the power, of itself, could not; in a way the physical wooden object, which never changed in any way other than when a coin was involved, could not. In some of the dreams I was an observer, in others, a participant. In this one I was somewhere between, as I took in the scents and sounds, blended with the textures while drinking of the dream's wretched visual offerings with perversely thirsty eyes. The images were the initial flash of the ignited match, assaulting my senses before I was even aware of my own presence within the dream. As the flame then settled into its cadence, the sulfurous vapor rose to meet the knowledge that I stood on the edge of a flat roof looking down upon urban squalor. Between stained dilapidated buildings, narrow lanes brimmed with mud, refuse, excrement, cows, pedal and motor driven vehicles, dark-skinned beggars and derelicts, stray animals vying for scraps of food. On one corner, beneath a rickety pole strung with blue bulbs, a man appeared to dicker with another over a scrawny monkey he held on a leash. On another a man prayed, hands in air, amid the puddle of the long garment he wore. Behind a set of stairs, and visible not only to my eye, a body wrapped completely in a sheet jerked at itself in violently persistent strokes, as if to find escape from its lot in that fleeting moment of bodily pleasure. Along the opposite side of the street three children poked despondently at the carcass of a dog that had apparently been struck by a vehicle. The stench that accompanied the snapshots was terrible, even from my location a few stories above street level. Its putridly sweet miasma doubtless pervaded the entire city, as much a part of its piteous character as the dense, suffocating, mizzly heat that dulled the wailing of car horns, melted the waste where it waited a collection that was not soon coming, and ultimately turned me away from the scene in nausea.

The picture I discovered behind me was the diametric opposite of the one that lay below. It would have been a paradise even in decent conditions, with its lush garden of exotic plants surrounding a tiled swimming pool of seductively clear water. In this place it was an oasis on the order of Eden. A cruel mirage summoned out of the entropic stew. If additional evidence to that effect was required, I needed look no further than the surface of the pool, which, though it did not stir in the laden air, produced the gurgle of moving water. A phantom song to go along with the coolness that washed over me as I stepped to its edge seeking any validation of my own existence in its illusory depths. The echo emerged, but not in the way, or even the context, imagined. It came instead off the barrier of putrefaction that encircled the roof. Or was it, on a closer listen, an echo at all? The source of the watery music now seemed to be in that direction instead of the pool. And underlying its gurgle, the faintest chuckle, a thing only partially heard at first but which then bled through the pattern of the water to find its own rhythm, a rising and falling that both complemented and contradicted the prominent layer. The subtlety of the duet, which remained subdued as it lured me from the poolside in search of its source, lent it a haunting, even sinister tone. The discovery before me, I knew, would be a terrible thing, a moment of enlightenment that would mean the dissolution of the setting in which it occurred, leaving me, the prop in that setting, forever lost among the ghost laughter. But it had to be known; otherwise what purpose, the dream?

Descending the three steps that appeared at the end of the deck required a suspension of perception, a coming to terms where there were none. The scene offered at this end of the roof, though even more meaningful than the corrupt streets my eyes had partaken of moments before, only vaguely registered. My focus was on the whirlpool now coming into the picture, the rim of its polished teak frame angled in such a way as to afford its user a prime view of the tiers of stairs depositing the rapturous bathers into the filthy river. I knew who leisured in the swirling water before she came into view. Nonetheless, I was unprepared for the rictus of her teak face looking up at me at angles to her neck, suddenly laughing maniacally at my having found her at the end of the moment—the eternal moment to which we are all, the lot of us, subject.

~

The last dream that I experienced before arriving at a vital crossroads in my relationship with my inherited power expounded on the first, and all that had occurred between. This one was actually more a vision than a dream, not because it occurred out of sleep, but because I witnessed its content as on a screen. There was a distance between me and the images as they unfolded, as though I were being shown something rather than living it—until the last, that is. The dream began with a view from a high vantage point. Below me fields stretched to a village beyond which, several miles farther out, stood the outline of a metropolis against a leaden sky. There was a chromium effect to it all, in this particular instance not of the cinematic sort, but as if the picture had been frosted by a passing mercurial fog which still hovered among the structures of the city, luminously outlining them where there should have been no distinction between earth and firmament. But it was a fool's scene, I realized, as people began to appear in the foreground, oblivious to any such phenomena. They went about the business of people, with their hoes and their sheep and their tractors, now their lawnmowers and neighbors and automobiles. The picture moved in that fashion, from an airborne perspective to an earthbound one, then alternating back again. The succession occurred less in frames than in the quasi-fluid stream of images caught in the half closed eye of an eagle delighting in the ascents and descents of its luxury; and less in a raptor's eye than in the dreamer's. For in spite of the effect of being a witness to a presentation, that knowledge was always present: that I dreamed, that I looked upon a world I could manipulate if I could find the right key. Yet there was no desire to search for that key. I knew it would come as it always did in these trips abroad.

Time, that dubious concept, proved me right as the mansions of steel and glass, the persons of iron and dirt converged into one functioning entity. That is when the sense of observing abandoned me and I became a part of the documentary. Perception yielded to proportion and proportion to perception as I realized that the camera had deceived: the activities on which it had been trained occurred, in relation to myself, on a different scale. With that realization, the lens suddenly zoomed in on a single magnificent object. As I beheld the thing I knew it in the way a man knows a pair of pants he has worn and been comfortable in for years. Yet this was no article of clothing, rather something even more familiar, even more personal. The object was made of teak, brilliantly polished like the whirlpool I had encountered during that other journey into intimate, inaccessible knowledge. It was inlaid with gold and ivory and jade, veins without order that mutually contributed to an exact aesthetic construct; a circulatory map to Truth the likes of which my art had only pretended toward. I approached it with both expectancy and expectation, wonder and prewritten awe, knowing that if I dared place my body within its embrace, I would have the answers I'd so long sought, answers that could fully translate a man. And yet I did not hesitate, *could* not do so. To deny it was to deny my own being. Unlike a limb, that can be severed, a nerve, anesthetized, the thing before me was coded into the genome of my soul. It did not call and I did not answer. We were already one, the throne and I. Its arms were my arms, its back my back, its illustrious chaotic designs my own.

As I took its embrace, there, mirrored in the sky in front of me, was my fresco. I sat melded into my seat, wholly revealed. The woody material of me, the solitary slot that gaped eagerly in my chest, the grotesque grin that wracked my face, spilling terrible laughter upon the microcosmic world below.

~

It was that laugh, finally, that brought me to my decision. Miss Teak, and with her, the power she had given me, must go. I phoned Francis and told her, to her effusive protestations, that I was finished with painting. What I would do with the remainder of my moment on earth, I didn't know. I only knew what I would do the next day, and that was toss Miss Teak, with bricks strapped to her body, into the Atlantic deep.

IV

Tomorrow never arrives though, does it? Strangers and unforgotten faces come calling, coins in hand. I knew it was the shopkeeper from Cochem before I opened the door, yet dared not peep through the hole before committing that inevitable act lest it be true. She stood there in the twilight in jeans and frock, like the seller of curiosities that she was, smiling that dreadful smile she had borrowed from Miss Teak. It occurred to me as I let her pass inside, uninvited, that we, Miss Teak and I, should have expected her long before. For she was the doll-puppet's puppet-doll as surely as I. The only difference between us was that she possessed the coin. That fact, I saw in her gaze, would soon be remedied.

"Have you read Theodore Sturgeon's 'Microcosmic God'? It is about a scientist who becomes like a god over his terrarium of miniature genetically bred people."

"I don't want to be God," I said.

"Oh, he wasn't God, make no mistake. He could create and destroy, but he could not change mortality. You, on the other hand, can. Like him, you are compassionate—indeed were selected for your sensitivity to the pain of the human condition. Unlike him, you can alter the otherwise inevitable path men are forced, according to the capricious designs of a lunatic creator, to endure. Have I told you where we finally found our Miss Teak? In Varanasi, India, lazing in a whirlpool overlooking the Ganges River and its bathers cleansing away their sins in the filth. She was laughing, laughing at all the rot, the deception, the misery and mayhem delivered by her. That is why you have no choice but to accept this coin. Because you can salvage the wreck she has created. You can make your world one that is fit to live in. A motion of your hand is all it would take. A motion as simple as that required to deposit a single coin toward a future that does indeed exist, despite your understandably cynical, exquisitely human appeals regarding the moment. Do you know the one place where the moment exists independently? In the wooden box where we imprisoned the being responsible for your cynicism. And even there she is not in a vacuum. What has been done and what cannot be undone again are always with her. That is the irony we thought she would appreciate."

Like the material of the box and the grin on her face, I thought as I stared at the coin resting dully in her open palm. But the gravitational pull of the point in space the coin occupied was specific. Wooden cages and rogue creators fell off the outer edge of its event horizon. I said:

"What I want to know is this: What difference does it make who fills the God role when the created know they can be snapped out of existence at any time? That's where the pain of existence truly lies, isn't it? That sense of inferiority and worthlessness abides in at least the subconscious of all religious people. For those who are not religious, the situation is equally as dire. We are either manufactured or we are not. Either way, one loses."

"But as God you can undo even that."

"What?" I said, sardonically. "The knowledge of doom or the doom itself?"

"Any and all, of course. If you prefer your creatures not think of themselves as created, then will it so. If you prefer they meet no end, then will that so. You are God, after all."

If there was a point in time and space where she suffered her downfall, it was then and there. Not in the arrogance inherent in the sentence *You are God, after all*, but in those words *your creatures*. In a moment I have only known in painting, when the amorphous suddenly and unexpectedly takes form, it all came clear to me. Those power limitations I'd encountered were not about safeguarding the world's ignorance, but keeping me from running away with my newly gained abilities. I was not here to assume Miss Teak's might but to restore it, in all its fury, to its owner. I was here to free her from her prison, to unleash her upon her creation again. The means to that accomplishment was through a vessel. A vessel with a hand for sweeping, a mouth for laughing, eyes for watching all the misery continue to unfold. I didn't know how, nor whether we were to share the same body or I was to be cast out of mine. What I did know was that the force in me was suddenly bristling at the thought of becoming one with her, as though it had secretly been growing with every cent dropped, biding its time quietly while waiting for its mistress's instruction. Though I was disgusted with myself for letting it blossom again, I did not confuse my weakness for lust. Not then. Not ever again. I would die first.

And yet, was my hand not even now reaching for the coin? Yes, and at my own bidding. For this was the only way—slim as that possibility was—of seeing the thing finished.

The instant before accepting it, I paused, looking up into her shining, hungry eyes.

"One question more before,"—the sarcasm came of its own—"becoming hers. Why all the drama? Why a thousand cents? Surely a hundred would have done. Or none at all. Why found coins? Do others not spend as well?"

She was grotesque, perverse, a grin with a face. "Mystique. Allure. There had to be a process, an involvement on your part. A preparation period. The idea of happenstance seemed a suitable tool for the task. There is the smell of destiny about it, of greater purposes. Even we are not immune to its allure. Even we are subject to its moods."

Yes you are, I thought as I took the coin from her. The power surged to a hectic pitch in me as I stepped over to where Miss Teak lazed against the wall amused by the whole affair, and deposited it in its slot. There was a period of nothingness, where even the screaming came to a halt; then, with the force of some alien super enhancer administered directly into the ghost, I swelled to the limits of my capacity, then out of myself, saturating and encompassing the room, the distances, the vast tapestry that is the moment.

It is a tapestry, as I behold it in its magnificence, whose overlapping scenes depict entire armies stopping in their tracks, realizing the inelegance of their ways; deadly weather systems brimming with anticipation at the prospect of landfall;

riotous cells retracting in shame from their eager mutinies; chemically deficient brains surrendering gleefully to the twisted road in front of them. A tapestry, as I behold it in its terrible splendor, whose superimposing depictions include hordes reveling in the glorious bath of spilt blood; deadly land-bound weather systems shying off to sea; riotous cells daring their brethren to join the cause; chemically deficient brains eschewing madness for the pursuit of alternate springs.

That same tapestry, that same moment which I continue to attest is all that exists as I stand laughing from my seat in a whirlpool, simultaneously burning this record into infamy and the lunatic Miss Teak and myself into furthest oblivion.

Elephant Speak

On the eighteenth day of December, in the year 2534, a ghost was born in Euristanbula for the first time in a century, and I was there to witness it. Blond hair, blue eyes, skin the color and quality of prayer wax, in stark contradiction to the dark complexion my wife and I and everyone else in the world share. My name is Saro. My son's name is Hayalet, of the old tongue meaning simply *ghost*.

I will never forget my wife's reaction when they hurriedly removed the frenzied babe from the delivery room. Through the mucusy film they didn't pause to wipe away, she caught a glimpse, a mother's intuitive glimpse, of the color of our new son before the nurse vanished through the doorway. Then my wife turned the naked discs of her eyes on me, as though to implore that the thing not be so. That is the second face to come across Leyla's normally calm countenance that I shall not forget.

The third occurred ten days later in an otherwise empty section of the neonatal unit that might have been reserved specifically for our son, in his strange capsule. He was neither premature nor ill, but the incubatory environment was deemed best for his unique situation. I remember vividly not only Leyla's face as she first beheld our tranquilized though still somehow recognizably feral son, but also the tremor that passed through her hand into my own body as we stood there together above the glass tube.

Her words were as much a contrast as skin color. "What are we going to do, Saro? They will want to *work* on him."

Of course there was nothing we could do. The ghosts appear two or three times in a generation at best, in various parts of the world. I once heard them likened to albinos of the past, but albinos were less rare, and a far easier trek along the genome. Not because of pigment, but because of behavior. Ghosts are born feral. As though they cannot tolerate a civilization that has bred them out through natural dilution. As though they awaken into life remembering something the rest of us don't.

Officials necessarily became involved and we were given no choice but to take Hayalet to the FDH (Facility for the Domestication of Humans) in Prague, the haunt of ghosts worldwide.

II

In the late twentieth/early twenty-first century, biologists in Russia and America performed extensive research on control groups of feral and domesticated mammals, seeking the answer to the question of whether Neolithic farmers sought specific qualities out of the mammal species they domesticated or whether tameness was the single criterion—in which latter case, all other benefits from the human perspective were side effects. Through the generational process of straining out and interbreeding human-tolerant specimens of wild groups of rats and silver foxes, it was learned that not only did the tame test stock become more amenable to humans, they also developed physical characteristics that differed from their wild cousins, such as droopy ears and white spots in their fur.

Additionally, the 'tame' specimens of silver fox seemed to be able to follow human gestures, like the dogs that had been domesticated from wolves before them. It was theorized that this ability had to do with the removed fear of humans, and led ultimately to a scientific breakthrough. If the process of certain genes in the neural crest cell were slightly delayed, the maturation of the adrenal glands that underlie the first fear response of young mammals might also be put in check. From there it was a matter of isolating the specific genes responsible for the timing of neural crest development, and addressing them accordingly.

Sadly, none of this could be made to apply to ghosts, which came out of the womb tortured—for lack of a better word. Tortured—for lack of a worse one.

The specific genes as addressed by science proved contextually meaningless. They better fit quantum theory than genetics, describing a chaos impulse that stuck like mud in parental hope. The ghost was a true Asimovian mutation in the vein of the Mule, only without the power, and the at least superficial tolerance for society.

III

Like the ghost he was, Hayalet haunted. He haunted before we had even seriously broached the subject of leaving him in Prague, among his kind—which meager unit totaled six without him: two born in Indochina, one in Africa Proper, one in the Polynesians, one in the United West. And none expected to live beyond fifty years, though the average human lifespan was nearing one hundred. Unanimously, the parents had elected to leave their aberrational spawn there for the duration, with visitation privileges if they so chose.

Most of them, we were informed, did not so choose.

We decided against the grain. In terms not of visitation, but of actual guardianship. It was then we met Doctor Ekka. She said she had been looking for exactly the volunteers we, as Hayalet's biological parents, represented. If we would agree to let the lab periodically observe the Caucasian (we cringed at this derogatory term, but recognized its place as a scientific reference), then the State of Euristanbula saw no problem with the experiment.

Experiment? The keeping our own son at home? We agreed very much, they dispensed the necessary tranquilizers, and we returned home to Bucharest with our lab child. No, it wasn't so simple as that. There were months of bureaucracy to endure, faces to pretend to talk to, forms to shuffle, clouds to convince. We remained steadfast, and eventually the fog cleared and a plane came in, bearing a child whose eyes were the blue of a vagabond tongue of fire rather than an iris or an afternoon sky. Fortunately for us, we had all three in our house; we burned symbolic prayer candles as easily as we watered the irises or remembered the afternoon sky. Conversely, *he* had the advantage of viewing *us* through the still clinging film of his freak birth.

Against all advice Leyla managed to massage milk from her all but dried up breast, and tried to feed him.

He tore her nipple with his gums and newly cutting teeth. Screamed from his eyes.

Experiment indeed.

IV

The candles are sculptures, things of the past: Mosques, Cathedrals, Temples. They burn as though remembering the past, his eyes, dripping what is life into a pool that would be blood in another context. Leyla claims to have some sense of him, but I know it is a mother's wishes. What sense of him I have takes ominous forms.

I dreamed once as I fell asleep with his wearied, ever reluctant body at my chest. I'd meant to place him back in the pen, but his breathing somehow converged with my own and the moment slipped away. There were terrific concussions, superimposed seas of blinding radiation, sands and rivers and skyscrapers blown to obscurity. There were skies, white, Caucasian, ghostly. Great bloated serpents spinning among them, spreading oily darkness from their mouths wherever they flung. There were people. Clowns standing on top of wheeled machines, grasping the spewing hoses in their fists, laughing at the seminal saturation of the sky.

He woke with me, the surviving petals of unpolluted firmament returning to their original azure as they converged into twin vortexes. I hated him that he terrified me, but loved him that his exotic eyes gazed at me before peering about in anticipation of the next mood fix. One wonders what might happen if such a fix were withheld from so fierce a creature as a son.

I didn't tell Leyla. She was only his mother after all.

I did tell the lab techs when they next visited. Although the dreams were indescribably personal, I felt that anything, however peripheral to the core, which might improve my son's condition was worth the exposure.

V

It is endlessly slow, the wax. Through the window in his cage, Hayalet took to watching it melt over whatever lay in its path. We, regrettably, took to his tranquilizers. There had been that caveat at the outset—"If you keep him, you may find yourselves on tranquilizers as well"—but we'd ignored the opinions of scientists, in favor of psychologists, in favor of naturalists. We'd ignored so much. We ignored nothing now as he grew from babe to boy in the essential cage supplied by the FDH.

The Facility's lab techs came and went with increased frequency, as if they expected that at any moment Hayalet would abandon what docility he had demonstrated in his drug-controlled state and slash my wife and me to ribbons. One afternoon, in another dream dreamed with my son, a knife capable of such materialized. The technician held it up so that I could see its serrated edge against a harsh glare that my dream sense likened to the effulgence trained upon my wife's vagina as she spilled forth Hayalet into eager hands representing the fold of mankind.

As Leyla entered the stage as a separate cognizant fixture in the chromium reality, the tech turned the blade just so, studying the edge, drawing from its energy before embarking on ceaseless questions. Did we think the Caucasian would do himself harm? Did we think he would do *us* harm? How could a kitchen knife have landed in his room? Had we allowed him to eat with us in an unsecured location like the dining room? Had we dined with him in his own room? Was he eating meat? Were we not sticking to the vegetarian diet prescribed?

Hayalet's heart drummed against mine, though he was too old now to cradle to my chest. I woke from my melted posture in the easy chair we keep in his room to find him looking at me from his poised position on his bed. It passed through my mind that he might strike. Such a notion hadn't occurred to me in at least a year.

I motioned for him to lie down. After some moments he obeyed, into an extravagant flood of piss whose smell, as it exceeded his diaper, alerted me as always to a humanness that was as often lost in a mist of science.

Much like the cluster of genes they could name but could not rename.

VI

When he turned four a contingent of higher level FDH officials, including Doctor Ekka herself, arrived with an unprepared for surprise of a birthday present. Her name was Golge—of a tongue, *Shadow*, in keeping with our own use of Turkish in naming our son—she was three years old and had been genetically spliced from Hayalet and his mother upon our son's birth. Standard procedure with the Caucasians, Ekka said. Environments must be formed. Parameters changed. Interactions observed. Sites along the genome compared. Old beakers replaced with new. It all might have boggled the mind if Leyla and I weren't already acclimated to the FDH's Elephant Speak and clinical indifference to our own needs.

Of course we accepted Golge with—hesitantly—open arms. Forget that the officials would have insisted on it anyway. Forget that she seemed almost gentle as she absorbed her new surrounds through heavily dosed sable eyes set in soft almond skin. We had already accepted one anomaly into the neatly woven fabric of our lives. We weren't going to turn away another, blood of our blood, however difficult it might have been to specify which relation in the family unit she occupied.

Indeed, any specifications came from the FDH. Modifications upon previous modifications were made to our home, so that his cage abutted hers, a clear resin wall separating the two. The sole difference in their environments was that only she had the ability to open and close the door in the synthetic barrier. When we voiced our skepticism they assured us no harm would come to either of them. They were both internally equipped such that any physical contact between them would result in an unpleasant electrical charge passing between them. As the cages had no free objects lying about that they might hurl at each other if the tranquil state broke down, they could—and in Prague, did—coexist.

Welcome to the calm skies of our household then, *Shadow*. Let the experiment continue in all fervor.

VII

On the fourth day, amid the lava-like dance of prayer wax, she opened the door. Leyla saw it on the monitor in the kitchen and literally screamed my name. This action on Golge's part was an event, to be certain. The FDH techs had told us to expect a month at minimum, given that the fear response in even half ghosts dwarfed other emotions, e.g. curiosity. Add to this that Golge's response to Leyla and me, her providers, had been less than familial—and that she must have smelled Hayalet's temper bleeding through the barriers on some level—and a snarling recipe conspired in the pot.

For Hayalet's part, at first he merely stared in apparent fascination. Leyla and I watched on the screen, not daring to interfere with whatever developed. His sister approached like a Clarke image as interpreted by Kubrick. He was the monolith and she was the ape. Her hand, as it explored the air before him, seemed to shine with his own radiance. His mouth moved and she immediately withdrew her hand. He in turn recoiled at her action. My wife and I were witnessing a single presence, one that wished to be reunited with itself but was unsure how.

While watching this in my own trance, it occurred to me suddenly how vicious our interpretation of viciousness. How alien. As though we had arrived at its discovery from far away when in fact the primal fire, that snarling recipe conspiring in the pot, had bred us all.

In their now merged cage Golge and Hayalet communicated without ever touching, his lips hovering over her ear in potential revelations that Leyla and I had only dreamed of extracting from him—not least because *he had never spoken a single word in our presence.* The two were signs to each other in the universe, it was clear to me, neither caring how they had come to be in the company of the other, neither wishing for more than was given—whether that gift be confession, conciliation, or conspiracy.

On the sill of the kitchen window, the wax dripped palely, like the skin of a literary corpse.

VIII

Who are you people? I wanted to ask Hayalet and Golge. I wanted to wax existential, but the purposes and ideals inherent in so futile an exercise restrained me. Still the prayers melted. Still my children—may I call them that?—came to be comfortable with each other, though some random, shared chemical kept them abreast of the fact that physical contact remained taboo.

We do not believe in an ancient Allah as we burn our prayer wax, Leyla and me. We also do not believe in specters. What *do* we believe in? The F in FDH is for the Facilitation of that grand question. I believe in the possibility that my son may live beyond fifty. I believe in the possibility that his ferity is permanently suppressible, with time. I believe that Leyla believes. In that I do.

So who were they then, our Hayalet and Golge? Where had they come from?

What was their purpose? If their hides were membranes stretched over drums, what ear to hear but that of the dancer, who does not distinguish between ghosts and shadows as she fulfills her dance? Ivory, honey, bone, coffee, milk, ebony, wax, they all dissolve into the earth eventually. What value, one freak and one half freak, in the progression of humankind? I was naïve, yes, but I didn't have to blindly accept that droopy ears weren't intrinsically elephantine, in the way of FDH's Elephant Speak.

There was something beneath things. I decided, one night when we stayed awake watching the strange interactions of our children,that the only way to it was through Doctor Ekka. At least we had a name there, a somebody of some involvement. I contacted her the next morning, demanding to know why anyone in Prague cared.

All arrayed in her glimmery doctor uniform, she was a ghost, herself, there on the screen. "We care because we are scientists. We care because he is a boy without identity. We care because he is a boy. Believe it or not, we care for that reason."

I chose "or not" and asked about his sister. Why did Golge have to be involved? Weren't the "siblings" in Prague enough to write the record?

"There are no siblings in Prague," she said plainly. "Golge is the only such addition to our research. We developed her after hearing about your dreams. If your empathy response is so strong, think of what hers must be."

"Then you lied."

Her image seemed to tense with her features.

"We are not in that business, Saro. Sit still. I will be on the next flight out of Prague."

Saro. She didn't even have the clinical decency to eschew familiarity.

IX

"It is theorized that in the direst hour of what we now refer to as the Century of Uncertainty, when the survival of the human species was in the balance, bloodlines were genetically altered to breed these ghosts. A code was installed that modern science, which we like to think of as superior, thus far has been unable to break—though there is some solace, I suppose, in knowing that hiding a thing is much easier than finding a thing."

Ekka and I sat in the kitchen in front of the monitor. Leyla had thankfully taken me up on my offer to tend to the children while she went to her parents' to relax a while. The stress in the house was both that palpable and malleable.

"Breed them why?"

She pretended to watch the nonactivity on the screen. "To be carriers of the crimes of the past."

I remembered dreams. Strange and terrible dreams. "But why? As some sort of punishment? That would seem as regressive as the ghosts themselves."

She abandoned any pretense now, looking at me squarely as she said, "So that *people might never forget*."

Dreams. Empathy response. Ferity. It all came circling back in the mind of science, bless such fortitude.

X

I happened to be watching on the evening Golge lay down to sleep beside Hayalet. The mundane chore of cleaning the kitchen fell immediately into the background as I observed him almost touch her as she turned to face away from him. In that aether the camera exploited, I saw a slight smile form on her face, a sweet something that seemed as hard to place as the tear that burned for release from my eye.

Though I'd have guessed to the contrary, they fell almost immediately into their medium, a comfort zone that was as palpable, and I hoped as malleable, as the stress that had so long pervaded the house. I left the world and its melting wax behind in favor of him, my son; them, my children. Being with them, a part of their experience, whatever its nature, whatever turn it took, was all that mattered.

Quietly entering the cage, I placed myself in the easy chair and invited all the science, all the data, all the input away. If tomorrow we woke cleansed only of wakefulness, then so be it.

If all I heard was Hayalet's whispering into my sleeping ear, *Sit still, father. I am on the next plane out of the wilderness.*

The landscape was vast, desolate, debris-strewn. Doctor Ekka approached out of it, a young silver fox perched on her shoulder looking at me curiously, without fear. When it began to speak, I woke suddenly, remembering I was dreaming, but then the stirrings of my children on their bed drew me back into the waste. It seemed to change before my eyes, length and breadth, scrap metal winds driven by destitution, observation. The sky full of oily black, the sun like a great swollen teat generating a milk of hopelessness.

The milk pooled into cloaks, and walls. Of doctors and their laboratories. Scalpels and syringes shined against waxen walls. The smell of liquefaction permeated everything as it oozed into the eyes and noses of every object in its path, stifling breathing, suffocating out any future, any past. I saw her rise desperately in response, seizing and clutching him through the hot sculptor of electricity, against his halfhearted struggles placing her ear against his mouth, and the world dripping eternally in its elephantine wax.

The Man in Window Three

Art imitating life? Veins had to stifle a laugh at the thought. He couldn't believe he was actually here, on display, occupying window three of Vileci's famous *Stations of Vitruvian da Vinci*. That a vagabond like Veins should assume one of the twelve poses of Icon's most highly regarded and valuable work of art was more than ironic—it was bizarre.

The idea had come to Veins when his friend Turtle returned from a week in incarceration bearing news of a roundup. Turtle and another man had been going through out-processing when they overhead an officer in an adjoining room talking over the com about it. It seemed the operation was going to be the most substantial of its kind in years, in anticipation of the arrival of the Fveldan czar on Icon. Not only did Turtle obtain the what, he also got the when, which set the wheels in Veins's head spinning. Knowledge like that, he told the Four Block gang, could not be allowed to go to waste. Sebastian had made the observation that avoiding a roundup could hardly be considered waste, but he was the youngest and so easily forgiven his naiveté.

The idea had begun to spread petals almost upon the moment of its birth. Veins was the one among the close-knit band of six who could see beyond the inevitabilities to action. Yes, the space station Icon, population exceeding two million already, was in a continuous state of construction, and yes, as long as the port swam with indigents to be rounded up for what amounted to slave labor, the authorities would continue to do so. However, alternatives to that fate could and must be created. Whenever he used the E word, they laughed at him, spurting their mantra about the insanely expensive cost of passage off Icon and the impossibility of stowing away, with the level of dock security as it was. He might have grown hopeless having to remind them over and over again that had fools not dreamed their dreams, mankind would still be carrying clubs. Instead, their fatalist speak kept him lucid and alert. He knew in the end it must be Escape.

Wielding his background in chemical science—a career path that had been cut short by ethical considerations—Veins managed to convince the gang to help him break into the built-in exhibit while the roundup was in progress. As convenient as the diversion was, it by no means solved all the problems associated with a bold scheme like this. In order to remove the contents of window three, which Veins had concluded was the one part of the display where the scheme could crystallize, the power flowing there had to be cut off. Ultimately, a guard had to be captured and interrogated. They learned enough from her to know that the power source was independent, which played into their hands perfectly.

When it was shut down, a sort of whine escaped the hominotron it fed, as if the thing were cognizant of its own submersion into torpor. Veins took his place without hesitation, the drugs in his body neutralizing the juice it was imperative his friends let flow again. In deep space, chemical power was cheapest and easiest, but it was also, by nature, susceptible to counteraction. The question was; would the lie sell? Would his skin shimmer to the satisfaction of the looker? Would his movements convince the eye of that inhuman perfection that characterized automatons? Would his eyes tell tales? It all remained to be seen.

The first bay in the three-kilometer stretch of Icon's port was the one set aside for visitors of highest distinction—hence the presence of Vileci's masterpiece. The twelve windows in which the Stations were sequentially depicted ran along one wall, number three being directly across the broad naked pad from a larger-than-life hologram of da Vinci himself, for whom Icon's galactic museum was named. To one side of the hologram was a rotating image of Leonardo's Vitruvian Man, while on the other was a sketch of the Roman architect and engineer, Vitruvius. Veins watched the images through eyes that were not supposed to see, wondering when someone would show up, putting his act to the test. Before disappearing with the others, Turtle had assured him none of the dock hands or security personnel would give him a second glance. It was the next ship into port—precisely what they were waiting on—that he should worry about, particularly if its occupants had never experienced Vileci's work of art. Veins knew he was right, but it wouldn't hurt his confidence to have even a disinterested audience.

As if manufactured by his thoughts, a uniformed janitor, broom in hand, emerged from a door in the opposite wall. The gray man glanced right and left as if to assure himself that he was the only one in the cavernous bay, then he lifted a foot and stepped right through the da Vinci hologram. Veins kept his amusement within, watching with the blind eyes of a dummy. The broom began to work, briskly, moving bits of nothing around in spaces already addressed by low-suction ventilation. It was as though the sweeper's vocation was to be a reminder of old Earth. And yet everything about him, not least his playfulness, precluded his being a robot.

Meanwhile we docksiders starve and share shipping boxes for homes, thought Veins. He had of course seen janitors about the docks, but he had never really observed them. Something about this one sang of absence of purpose, absence of…illusions. Hadn't Veins himself hired on for cleaning duty, only in other, more needy places? He wondered if he was suited for looking at the world through a window.

The janitor glanced up suddenly, finding Veins across the cold slab of the bay floor. Veins lowered his head, lifted it again, lowered it, lifted it…*It is done…It is done…It is done…*

The janitor approached, broom bristles trailing along the floor, the squeak of his rubber soles on the glassy-smooth surface saluting the bay's sharp acoustics. When he stood in front of window three, he stared directly at its occupant's eyes, which remained in a fixed position as Veins performed the repetitive motion over the otherwise immobile cruciform of his body. For a moment Veins thought the other might attempt to plunge a hand through the glistening security field to touch him. He wondered if this fellow longed to leave Icon too. In that second in the revolution when their eyes made contact, Veins was certain he detected a void beneath the mixture of suspicion and expectancy. He submerged himself in that amorphous, disturbingly familiar emptiness as a substitute for fear of discovery.

Soon the janitor's expression yielded to a shadow and he turned away. Window three could do no more for him than he could do for it. It perhaps had glowed with life for a moment, but that moment was gone.

The inertia resumed for the bay in general. As the man drifted out to the periphery of his periodic forward vision, Veins considered a possibility which the captured guard had confirmed to be less than slim—that the bay would remain empty until the next scheduled arrival of two days hence. In that awful event, the Fveldan czar would be looking upon the *eleven* Stations of Vitruvian da Vinci because Veins would have since collapsed. He chided himself for his imagination. He should be pleased; his first test had proved a confrontational one and he had passed it without event.

A male voice came from the rear of the bay, where the janitor had slipped from view. Veins resisted the impulse to glance that way, homing in on the words instead of their source. His control paid off, for the speaker walked as he talked. When the speaker came into view, enough had been said to render Veins surprised to find the janitor holding the com.

"Welcome to Icon, Sirus. Leonardo opens his arms to you. Object one is disabled, object two is currently abandoned as forecast. The bay itself is empty. Remain sheathed. Repeat, Sirus, remain sheathed until you are in the lock. No need to revert to secondary plan. Your approach has gone undetected. Leonardo opens his arms to you."

Veins didn't know what to make of this strange development. Who were these people who had dared approach the station invisibly? Whatever they had in mind, surely it could only aid the Four Block crew. Veins laid aside all other designs, poising for the moment. The com hovered in the janitor's hand, as if he considered saying more, then he hooked the device to his belt and strode towards the portal, which would open when the ship was in-lock and air generation complete.

It occurred to Veins that a third party had to be controlling the portals, or else the ship would not be able to dock. Since the janitor's back was to him, and obviously the bay wasn't currently being surveilled by human eye, he risked a glance up at the control station, some twelve meters aloft. Sure enough, someone moved within. The protruding enclosure had been as vacant as the rest of the bay when Veins took his position in window three.

The portal opened, revealing a small, sleek craft easily identified as a Sifter, manufactured right here on Icon. The vessel remained in the lock instead of entering, its opaque black shield concealing its cockpit. With his limited vision, Veins experienced what followed in intermittent frames. At a gesture from the janitor, the door opened and two persons, darkly clad and hurried, stepped out. One appeared to be the pilot, the other, judging by his bearing, master of the situation.

"I can't stand this cold, inorganic place," the latter told the janitor. "It's worse than being in the Sifter. I'll be glad to be out of here as quickly as possible."

"The Boor is in place?" said the janitor.

"It is. They'd better be cutting through the wall as we speak. How long now?"

The janitor gestured up at the control station. A woman's voice called down: "Twenty-five minutes."

Cutting through the wall? thought Veins. *Twenty-five minutes?* It struck him with the force of a hammer. These people were here for the Vileci.

It might have been his imagination, but he thought he detected the slightest tremor in the metal surrounding him. The wall in which the twelve alcoves were set divided this bay and the adjoining one. Had these people occupied bay two as well? Were they cutting through from the other side? *Boor*, the janitor had said. A Boor was an asteroid mining vessel, if Veins wasn't mistaken. It would possess the equipment to move and carry, say, *an entire wall.* How else could the thing be accomplished without compromising the integrity of the art?

A hum sounded as a door along the wall to Veins's right slid open. A voice preceded the person who emerged from the adjoining bay.

"We'll have it in the ship within fifteen minutes, Sirus. The acid laser is an amazing tool, silently slicing through construction metal like cheese. Step over and see her work."

"I saw her work on V-2, Creps."

"You didn't see her work on berian. She'll be through two meters of one of the hardest metals known before you can blink an eye."

"Fifteen minutes, Creps. Loaded and all."

"Right, boss." The door slid shut behind him.

How had these people known they would have the place to themselves? They were obviously professionals, having doubtless chosen this point in time with great care and planning—as Veins liked to think he and his vagabond gang had. It occurred to him that the answer to that question mightn't be quite as mysterious as seemed. When Turtle had stumbled on the information about the roundup, a man whom he hadn't known had been going through out-processing with him. For that matter Turtle himself sometimes had a loose trap. With the stakes involved here, anyone, including insiders, might have spilled. These were art thieves making off with one of the galaxy's most celebrated works of art.

Veins had no idea what he should do now. If he weren't the comrade he was, he would stay put and board the mining vessel with the rest of the stations of Vitruvian da Vinci. How simple that would be, escaping with the art. Of course they would very likely kill him when they found out the art and its value had been compromised—or would they? It struck him that he was as valuable to them as the thing they stole. The ring on his finger was a signaling device, and friends at the other end knew where the real contents of window three had been secured. Suddenly he knew what he should do.

It is done...It is done...It is—

The chemicals shimmered and sang as he stepped through the field trailing wires and apparatus like severed nerves. The motion drew all eyes, followed by mouths dropping in wonder and disbelief. Shaking off the sensation of being pulled back into place, Veins thought to say something profound, a smattering of humor for morale, but he and his crew were on as tight a schedule as these people. The words that came out of his mouth were:

"We seem to have a situation."

"I knew it!" announced the janitor.

"What is going on here?" demanded Sirus, the volume forcing an echo in the bay.

"What's going on is that you are about to steal the *incomplete* Stations of Vitruvian da Vinci." Veins reached behind him producing the object attached by adhesive to the small of his back. He leveled the weapon on Sirus. "Back off and

I would be more than happy to signal those who know where the missing part is." Without waiting for an answer, he touched the bottom of the ring with the thumb of the same hand. "They're on their way," he said. "Don't do anything stupid and we might be able to resolve this thing before unwanteds show up."

"Who are you?" said Sirus. "What's your fucking game?"

"Our game is to get off this hunk of metal. Our game is escape from Icon."

Incredulously: "So you sabotage a priceless work of art? Are you an imbecile?"

"An imbecile with the contents of the third station." Veins gestured behind him at the window, which looked ragged, gutted, now that he had stripped it of even its surrogate poser.

Sirus twisted his lips in disgust. "What you've done...it's blasphemous."

"Spare me," said Veins, looking towards the rear of the bay.

The Four Block gang, on cue, appeared in the door, weapons in hand, expressions transforming with surprise.

Turtle started to speak but was silenced by Veins.

"I'd like to take time for proper introductions," Veins said, "but I think we'd all like to get out of here as quickly as possible. Turtle, these are art thieves. They want the contents of window three. In exchange they offer us safe passage off Icon to wherever they are going. Right, Sirus?"

Sirus glared. "Get the art. We'll talk about it."

"I don't think so," Veins said. "Look, we're people with nothing to lose but our freedom, which we never had in the first place. You, on the other hand, have a fortune at stake. Do you really want to waste time?"

"Fine."

"Turtle, take Sebastian and bring back the art. The rest of you will go aboard—"

"No way," Sirus stated. "You produce the goods, then you come aboard."

Veins considered only a second. The gang might well be better off where they were. At least now they enjoyed the advantage of holding the bay under their weapons.

"Go," he told Turtle. Adding: "Quickly."

Turtle and Sebastian disappeared through the door. Veins looked up at the control station, found the oval of its occupant's face looking down at him. He turned to Sirus. "Earlier the lady said you had twenty-five minutes. Is there a specific reason for that schedule? Does something happen then?" The roundup would go on for hours, and he guessed the other knew it.

"Yeah. The lock opens and we're out of here. It's called efficiency."

Raising his voice so the woman at her station heard, Veins instructed Sirus, "Tell the lady to shut off all access between this bay and the next—" Too late as the hum sounded and the door in the wall slid open again. In two strides Veins was there, weapon extended in both hands. No one appeared against the backdrop of the gray hull of the Boor, all components apparently at work on the wall. Veins deduced the woman in the control station had opened the door in hopes of revealing the goings on in bay one. For whatever reason, communication between the two bays apparently wasn't doable. He leaned on the wall control, making sure his command wouldn't be overridden before turning back on Sirus.

He inclined his weapon in the direction of the booth as he said, "Do it. And while you're at it, tell her to set the exit portal to open five minutes from now."

Sirus stared at him. "No way."

"Five minutes," Veins said. "Unless she won't be going with us. In which case she's welcome to stay in the booth and open the lock when we're safely tucked away in the Sifter. Which, I assure you, will be within five minutes."

"I don't care for the *us* talk, friend."

Veins stepped to him, pushing the weapon in his face. "Guess what, asshole? I don't care whether you care for it or not. Now do it!"

Sirus looked up at the booth, and nodded.

Veins gave it less than a half minute, then ordered her down. She had just reached floor level and was stepping off the pad when Turtle appeared, followed by a two-meter-long, disintegrating shipping box, then Sebastian trying to hold together the tail end. Before they cleared the door, a shout sounded in the corridor behind them.

"You there! Where are you going with that?"

"Oh fuck," said Sirus.

"Run!" Veins yelled at his comrades. Automatically, he swung his weapon on the one person outside the gang who mattered at this moment—the pilot.

Turtle and Sebastian dropped the box, spilling its contents on the floor. As they tore past Sirus, his eyes never left the twisted, marionette-like thing. Veins watched him as he ushered the pilot, the janitor, the woman from the control booth, the gang, one by one, into the vessel. "Come on damnit!" he shouted.

But Sirus wasn't coming without window three. As he hoisted the hominotron up into his arms, one uniform followed by another appeared in the door, weapons drawn. At the same moment two fiery seams appeared in the wall housing the Stations of Vitruvian da Vinci, a long undulating moan escaping the separating metal. The security men, unable to believe their eyes, merely stared in wonder as the wall sank backwards, so smooth in its retreat as to leave the art's integrity perfectly intact.

All except window three, which Sirus clutched in his arm like a wounded lover as, at last, he put his attention on getting to the waiting Sifter. Veins held his breath, knowing that at any second the security men were going to overcome their stupefaction and turn on Sirus. Eternity seemed to intervene as Sirus crossed the threshold into the lock, such that by the time he inhaled the aroma of escape, the five minutes had expired and the inner portal engaged. As its door slid closed, the hominotron's leg caught on the lip and was pulled from Sirus's grasp. Veins shouted at him to let it go, but Sirus ignored the warning, managing to free the thing at the last second. Unfortunately, that second consumed a full one third of the lull between the closing of the inner port and the opening of the outer. The last thing Veins saw as the Sifter's door closed, sealing him in with the others, was Sirus's head fall to his chest.

It is done.

Transtexting Pose

The doorbell rang a second time. I called downstairs asking my wife to get it, but then the pipes bled in and I realized she was showering. I set down the newspaper and walked down the stairs in my socks, noticing as always that the empty spot on the wall in front of me desperately needed a picture or some other decorative object. It was a drizzly Saturday morning with no responsibilities but to the coffee-stained columns of recycled world events, the unexpectedly lurid paperback I'd been reading, and a crisp new deck of virtual cards that Luce and I had finally saved up the cash to purchase.

Ours was an old unit with a door that sported an actual peephole—which Luce will tell you is quaint if you're not looking at her squarely. Through the hole I saw three little girls in identical khaki uniforms standing there all in a row. I opened the door immediately so as to leave them stranded no longer in the arduous desert of their mission. What were they selling? Did it matter?

My first thought as they said, "Hello," almost in chorus, was that they were awfully *alike* looking, even for such a 'pale' corner of our beloved diverse city. Then one of them went solo, reaching forward to collect an object from beside the door, where she'd presumably placed it so that it wouldn't detract from the vision of three little girls all in a row.

The object was metallic silver and about the size and shape of a laptop, though considerably thinner. When she turned it, I saw its similarities to a laptop didn't end there. Metallic silver described just the back side of it. The front looked much like a lit LCD screen, containing a scene very simple in subject matter and obviously meant to convey the conceptual. Indeed, the sense I had was of conceptual art within conceptual art. The image itself was even free of frills or gimmickry, portraying a rowboat on an expanse of sea whose only other interruptions were three dark smudges in the distance that impressed me as islands. While it seemed reasonably safe to assume the picture was digital, it was impossible to tell whether the work was the product of a camera or a traditional artist—or both.

As though the wall at the foot of the stairs cared.

"And what do we have here?" I said, conscious of my flagrant adultishness.

"We are selling these for our project," said the girl who held it like a sign in her small hands.

"Oh?" I said. "And just what might that project be?"

"Transposing text."

Transposing text?

"Really? Sounds like a complicated project for a little girl." *Condescending*, I scolded myself. *Children do not like being condescended to.*

These children didn't seem bothered in the least. The one in the center spoke this time, as she pulled what resembled a business card from a pocket in her khakis: "We only need to raise five hundred dollars and we get a trip to the World's Fair in Los Angeles."

"Its theme," said the third girl, "is 'Our Virtual World.'"

I looked at the card. Though spare in content, it was quite nouveau in design. The words **transposingtext** repeated in a single horizontal line across the card, casting mirror shadows of the letter sequences **tra** and **si** and the single character **x**, so that the reflection read **art is x art is x art is**, etc.

"If we raise the money, we will have our own booth and our own sub theme: 'Redefining Man and God.'"

"Los Angeles," chimed in her neighbor, "is the City of the Angels."

"And what organization do you girls belong to again?"

They pointed to the card in my hand.

Transposing text. Art is x is art.

"How much for the…"—I was becoming slightly disoriented, which wasn't helping fill the empty spot on the wall—"the thing you have there?"

"Picture," said girl number one. "Twenty-two dollars."

At first I registered *Picture twenty-two dollars*. Then: Wow. Whatever happened to cookies. I fetched a twenty and a five out of my wallet and told them to keep the change. Man and God could always use some redefining.

Closer inspection confirmed that the image could not be distinguished from a screensaver. To me it was a remarkable medium. To others—that would be my wife Luce—it was a tackiness of the order of a velvet Elvis or Jesus, which violations were already sorely remembered in our house through the musical band *Felt Pelvis & Christ*, which I wouldn't let her expunge from my somewhat extensive collection. No matter, it was what it was, and that was, to fulfill the desolate need of the space at the foot of the stairs. In that endeavor, it was the better of every other work of art we'd tried there, namely her father's Army photo and my artist-signed and limited typewriter art image of Stephen Hawking looking at what might have been the very black hole Luce would not let him fill.

I had to hang it with two plate magnets, as it offered by way of accessory nothing but the fingerprints of the trio that had sold it. Which of course suited its neo-whatnot conceptual design. Luce would no doubt roll her eyes at that assertion, remembering my obsession with finding a way to keep the picture aloft. *Aloft*. Yes, that rather captures the sense of it as a floating thing, there on the wall, into whose meaningless simplicities my wife would sometimes catch me staring.

II

I am in a wooden boat with iron oarlocks, rowing. Before me is an island; above me, *aloft*, an airplane no larger than an albatross, throwing its shadow on the metallic silver water. I am looking for something but cannot remember (if ever in fact I knew) what. Where the image of it should be, there is near emptiness, the suggestion of a line here, a corner there. But the configuration itself, the proportions, remain shapeless. Unknown.

The island approaches steadily and the aircraft above me coasts at little better than my own pace, as if as lost as I. It occurs to me as I watch it lift on a vagrant wind that if it cruised at higher altitudes, it might seem a bird to the casual eye. Maybe that is what it was designed to do, to deceive the eye by flying outside the radius of dependable discernment, to seem a soaring bird when it is actually about darker business. That it glides low for me may simply speak to a malfunction, a random caprice of its mechanics. I doubt so. There is purpose here, dark or otherwise.

When I arrive at the island's shore, it seems I have been rowing for hours, but then, maybe mere moments. The bird enters the tree line beyond the recessed beach as I am stepping into surf that does not startle my naked skin. I am clothed in shorts, khaki, nothing more. The air is neither warm nor cool, the sky neither blue nor gray. There is no discomfort except in the shape that will not complete itself in my mind. I feel I will recognize it when I find it, but where to look? Here, this island?

I walk across the sand in the direction the bird has gone. Only a short distance into the trees—short, long, all such terms being relative—I find a clearing, and within it, the landed aircraft. As I approach the plane, figures begin to materialize around me out of the very aether. People. More specifically, black people. Black people in street clothes, denim bags pooling around their basketball shoes. Gangsta types tapping chests, chillin', discussin'—the rap materializing as smoothly and unobtrusively as the rappers. As with my contact with the water, there is no shock. There is only the realization, and the medium which they and I now share, though it is evident to me that they are unaware of my presence within it.

I have stopped, I realize, as I watch them gather around the airplane. One reaches down and opens a hatch on top of the fuselage and pulls from it a clear plastic bag. I step closer, imagining for a moment it might contain what I am looking for, but no, it is full of cylindrical glass containers of clear liquid. Test tubes are assuredly not what I am looking for, though associations of conformity, of rounded edges, do occur to me as the chatter of my unlikely companions fades in.

"This looks like some good muthahfuckin' shit."

"God*damn*, that's gotta be a couple ounces *at least.*"

"Break out da pipes, my niggas. We fixin' t'git fucked up on this shit."

Pipes. Pipes in the walls. Fading in. Bleeding in.

Only these aren't pipes in the walls, these are glass pipes, test tubes. The person holding the bag passes out the cylinders one by one to his bloods, then motions with a lift of his chin to a freshly materializing set of denim sags, who steps forward with a handful of what look like sacrament wafers. The brothers file up, uncapping the tubes, and he commences to crack the wafers over the open bottles, the whitish bits of matter dissolving in the liquid. As the last man gets his dose, the whole gang toss back the revised contents of their cylinders, gargling for a moment or so before spitting the reprocessed fluid back out, some into their empty tubes, others onto the ground.

This accomplished, the chorus lifts its collective head and begins to sing in the voice of angels, a music that strikes me as some soaring contract between Heaven and the 'Hood.

Meanwhile, the man with the crumbled wafers collects the tubes from the choir. He pulls out his cock and pisses into the empty cylinders then returns all the tubes to the bag from which they came, stuffing it in the plane's empty cargo compartment. The aircraft hums to life again, the chorus subsides, and in the relief, the bewondered voices of its tenors and basses expressing:

God*damn*, this is some muthahfuckin' good shit.

"And they are brothers, all?" says the insipid white face before me. "No sisters?"

"No sisters." I look around at what is an office. A desk stands between me and the insipid face.

"What does this say to you?"

"I'm not exactly sure. What does the fact that they are gargling angel water say to you?"

Words out of my mouth, just like that. It seems we've covered the story itself, the insipid white face and me, and we're now looking at deconstruction.

"The pipes," says it. "What do the pipes mean to you?"

"Pipes… You mean the tubes?"

"You said they were smoking prophylactics out of glass pipes."

I hesitate.

"Don't think about it. Just respond. What do pipes mean to you?"

Pipes. Pipes in the walls.

"My wife has a set that would offend God himself."

"Does she use them often?"

"Only when she is in the shower. Or one of her Catholic youth choral nightmares. Or on airplanes."

"You jest," says the insipid face.

"Do I?"

"Airplanes. Let's go back there for a minute. Can you describe the miniature aircraft in a little more detail?"

"I can," I say, wondering why the comparison is only now dawning on me, wondering why I'm speaking in present tense. "It's like one of those search and reconnaissance camera planes that law enforcement got from the military. You know, the ones operated by remote control."

"Oh, you mean like this?" An insipid white hand opens a drawer and pulls from it what looks very much like a remote control, points it at me and with an insipid white thumb, presses—

III

I am in the boat again, iron oarlocks creaking as I row. The plane practically hovers, itchingly so, above me. A new island approaches. The indistinct, amorphous sketch in my mind fails to fill out. Will I find this seemingly so significant, so (dare I say) *crucial* thing on the approaching shore?

My mechanical companion suffers an elongated shiver in advance of forsaking its painstakingly reflective pace for the island ahead. As it does I look for a camera eye, any sign of deception, but none is to be found in its smooth, metallic silver underbelly. If the machine possesses landing wheels, the seams of their compartments are invisible. Still, it propels fearlessly into the tree line, leaving me to splash blindly in the surf, across the sand, into the trees again.

Where are they? I know they're here. Not brothers this time—*others*. For among this fresh party voices occur in advance of mouths, flaunting a flippant femininity, with vivacious boas tossed ostentatiously over their sashaying syllables.

"Robbie, if sluts were apples, you'd be the reddest one on the vine."

"I hate to bust your *cherry*, Harvard, but apples don't grow on vines and your metaphors won't even buy you a quick trip to the bathroom with me."

Came a new voice (if one could be distinguished from the other): "Keep talkin' like that, Robbie girl, and you're going to get your dose of *this* cock before the shipment even gets here."

"Like I'd let a diseased gorilla like you rawdog me—*well, speak of the Devil with a tube dress on!*"

I close my eyes, open them again and there it is, the whole masquerade party right in front of me. With lavish loquacity and luxurious lashes, they flock to the aircraft, popping open the hatch as if it were a fresh can of mod and holding the baggie up into the limelight filtering in through the leafage above. This time I don't bother hoping for discovery as I move to better view the dispersal of the bag's contents. I do because I do, and the wonderment comes extra.

The tubes are smaller than before, in vial form, like those that contain Holy Water.

My wonderment does not end there as the silks and the stockings slide off and the boys splash their cocks with the sassy sacrament and head off into the trees in pairs and sometimes threesomes, leaving one aching materialization to plant the next baggie in the plane's compartment.

"'One pass to heaven'? Isn't that a bit obvious?"

The insipid face, with now a freshly vapid *expression.*

"I've said nothing about heaven," I return.

"Haven't you? How do you feel about heaven?"

"Heaven to me is some sexless guy with a restrictive collar."

"Sex. That is an interesting word."

"So is sexless."

"Do you believe that priests, in today's environment, are sexless?"

"I personally have not had sex with one."

"Let's go back to the restrictive collar, shall we? Isn't that a description you used for the three little girls?"

"I said they were wearing khaki uniforms buttoned to the collar."

"But you do have a fixation with priests," says the face. Vapidly. "May we say that at least?"

IV

Priests. That is what they are, certainly; virtually a coven of them as they loiter about the aircraft as over some first sacred text delivered from abroad. Not one among them seems willing to open the hatch, but all tremor with anticipation, relish. I drift close this time, for the image in my mind has begun to gel, still without proportions, but with phantom effusions of matter. *Dark* matter, as I think of it at this particular moment. Still in sketch form, but with conversely ominous and wonderful possibilities.

I watch them as they open the hatch, the bag, before turning to the wilderness as if waiting for the stimuli. I cannot put an exact name to the bag's contents nor an inexact face to the potential stimuli, though the former have harder edges than previous cargos. The priests cross their breasts with trembling fingers, their eyes are on the forest, not the strange bottles they hold poised under their forefingers. These, the coven of them, are incarnations before words. Strangled whispers from choked throats. Extended hands into nothingness.

I can almost see. I can almost see what it is that's withheld from me, but the very idea that it is withheld obscures its being. I find myself lost suddenly, without cranky oarlocks, without vapid faces, without even the brine (did I describe the brine?). The coming *unfolding*, the folding *uncoming*, does not involve me, even as the witness. It is its own occurrence...

They appear, maybe the children of other ages, other dimensions. Their hands do not extend to accept what the divine witches hold poised in their delicate hands. They look shyly on, one behind a set of glasses with a cracked lens, another the choral angelics that audibly and visibly cradle his head. But the witches extend nonetheless, with what are perfume bottles in their magic hands, now sprayed wrists that bear the sweet fragrance. Come, say they, and they heal with a spray of their perfume, the cracked lenses, the speakers through which suddenly I hear rock music—no, more like crack *rock* music, flavored with a bit of battery acid. *Felt Pelvis Christ* upon the scene, sirens open.

Indeed, what pipes for the children as they shyly, bewilderedly recall their heavenward glances for their earthward ones, then ashamedly slink away with the collars into the trees, already retching from the intake.

The pipes in the walls. The noises bleeding in as though to catch Luce jerking pictures from parchment walls at the foots of stairs. I know her, and I know that would be much of her. Then where? Where is the thing that inspires such…

"Surely you see," says it. "Surely, such cautious wings have not misguided you. What sound, your wife's, as she sings in the walls? Angelic? Demonic? Sweet? Sour?"

The sound of oarlocks as I press behind collared witches and children into the trees. Ahead, there are structures. Compact, rectangular, upward structures as though heaven just there. I watch disappearances within. Through a peephole I only now see in the door. Is it an eye at last to what I have been seeking? I look within, imagining for a fragmented second three little girls, but then witness the witch offer the boy a golden nugget, as might be used in a—

The small circular window cracks in response.

I look through the tri-parted hole and find in one fragment a brother's lips around the stem of a glass pipe, a melting condom in its bowl; in another, a sister's hands tying pink bubblegum around the perforated card stock she's wrapped around her cock, the words *One Pass to Heaven* disappearing in a spiral that might be a tongue around a pipe, a boy's eyes as he beholds the luminously golden nugget that is being presented him.

Promise of something that delights when inhaled, that numbs when exhaled, that dissolves when regarded. Indeed, what pipes for the children as they shyly, bewilderedly recall their heavenward glances for their earthward ones.

"Promise. That is where it begins. And you have proven your worth." The face, the hand pulls from the drawer the what. And in that moment the proportions fill out, the angles and the curves manifest themselves… though the thing itself is only a lump. A formlessness of clay.

"What will you do with it?" the insipid face asks.

"I will sculpt," I tell it.

And set about fashioning three little peddlers in khaki uniforms…

Glitzing With the Big Delicious

On the morning of Dandelion's birthday, which also happened to be the day I was to settle up with the Big Delicious, Hello had a *glimmer*. I had just blown out the candles—all but one of them, that is—when I caught the hint of it in my peripheral, lazily circling Hello's head like an uncertain halo.

It was momentarily forgotten as the lad reprimanded me for my lack of wind. "I warned you not to miss any candles," he said, frowning at the lone flame still burning among the thirty-one sticks of wax. "Dandelion could lose her wish."

"Hello, I don't even know what her wish would be."

"A violent death to the Big Delicious. What else?"

"I won't deny that's a fine choice, but how is *her* wish supposed to come true when *I* am the one blowing out the candles?"

"You're acting in her stead," he said.

In more than one capacity, I thought. As I started to add more to the conversation, he put his hand up to stay me, face assuming a faraway look. I remembered the *glimmer* the second before it appeared in his eyes, the revelation spreading across his features as he stared at me over the cake and its last, stubborn flame.

"You won't have to settle up with the Big Delicious," he said.

"Why?"

"Because Dandelion's wish is going to come true."

"What do you mean?"

"I mean he'll be a goner before his evening snort."

"That can't be, Hello. Look who we're talking about."

"I'm telling you, Zen, if you go to the Coral Mansion to make good with the Big Delicious, you'll be giving your money to a ghost—whether he still has a heartbeat or not."

"If you're wrong, Delicious's goons are going to dismember me." But I knew he wasn't wrong by the intensity of the *glimmer*, still orbiting his scalp net, yet to be released by his brain's enhanced electromagnetic field.

~

It wasn't as though I were settling up for myself anyway. The debt belonged to Dandelion, rest her soul. I just happened to be her surviving spouse and as such—at least in the Big D's bulbous eyes—the one upon whom the obligation fell. Not that I could blame Delicious for protecting his assets; he really had no choice but to enforce the deadline Dandelion herself had suggested. She was a fool to have imagined he would not do so because it fell on her birthday. What Dandelion wasn't as a wife, she *was* in recklessness. To the accusation and epithet "degenerate gambler" she inevitably responded with: "If I'd been born two years later, I wouldn't be in this mess." As if a scalp net was the fucking lottery.

We all might have been born a few years later. The Big Delicious might have been born a single week *earlier*. Outside of the test subjects, he was after all the first person to be equipped with a scalp net. And whoa the example he set when he reached 'maturity' and his net was activated, revealing the *glimmer*s. He didn't merely *experience* them to his appetite's content, he also ingested them, snorted them, shot them into his veins until he could scarcely be distinguished from any other humongous amorphous phosphorescent mass. He became the repository for all the premonitions, déjà vus, and instances of deeper knowledge that Vestibule's citizens experienced. He was a worm glutting on luminous soil, turning its energy back into waste in the form of fat.

The *idea* behind the scalp net meant nothing to him. He had been chosen to blaze the path because of the high level of electrochemical activity in his brain, not because of his interest in the pursuit of science. He didn't care one whit about the theory that all living things were interconnected through the planet's electromagnetic field, nor that this might answer such mysteries as why intimates sometimes read each other's thoughts or shared each other's dreams. He expressed as much to Dandelion when offering her a dose of his newest method of *glimmerglitzing*, as he so garishly put the act of feeding his craving. To her credit she declined to snort the *glimmers* adhering to the bald head sticking out of the conductor tank, happy to pocket her parlay earnings from the weekend's Mannequin Ball and be on her way.

~

"Will the Big D's goons come collecting when he is dead?" I asked Hello, that one flame still murmuring over the white and blue cake like the last dance.

"I'm sure of nothing except that he will die, today, and you don't want to give away your money."

I was satisfied with that. The sum, which amounted to all my savings plus all the credit I could get, insisted I be satisfied with that. I wanted to know if we should just wait around for the inevitable or go do something.

"Like what?" Hello said.

"Arena?" I suggested.

He tilted his head as if to say he was surprised at me.

"What else is there to do anymore, Hello?" The subtext the lad knew: No more movies because you young people won't buy, having seen too many fragments in advance to make the pictures interesting anymore. Can't go out to eat because the healthier spots are all overbooked. Can't play racquetball because the winner has often been decided before entering the court. No wonder Dandelion got involved in the Mannequin Ball, the one sport where the participants themselves cloud the outcome.

"Better we just stay quiet," Hello said. "What time is it?"

"Ten past eleven."

"They're coming. I hear them…in my net."

"Who? What are you talking about?"

"They don't know the Big Delicious is on his way to the Coral Mansion on High. They're coming for the money."

"You said—"

"I said the Big Delicious is a ghost. That's all."

"Damn, Hello. We've got to do something."

The knock came. More a pounding than a knock.

"We'll have to kill them," he said.

"How?"

Two *glimmers* of extra-origin began snapping around his head. He toyed with one for a moment before settling upon an action. "I will convey the premonition of their own destruction."

"Which is…forthcoming?"

"If it is foreseen, it is forthcoming."

The subtleties of that wisdom were beyond my netless mind. Nor did I care to be enlightened as I clung to a reinvigorated hope that I could somehow save my money as well as avoid an audience with his majesty's phosphorescent jelly.

~

Dandelion didn't know, though I did, that she was becoming a mannequin herself. It could have been the sauce, yes. It could have been the stress and malnutrition associated with her increasing gambling habit. Indeed, it could have been some other illness contracted along her wayward journey. But I knew. I like to tell myself that I knew before the scientists themselves knew what the deficiency of intuition/insight/sixth sense was doing to the non-equipped thirties demographic. To the older crowd it didn't matter. They had expended their share of cosmic enlightenment. A déjà vu to the dulled senses of a forty-year-old is more akin to nostalgia.

It is certainly true that after a time I had an inside to the Big Delicious that the scientists no longer had due to his foreknowledge of any and all attempts to access him. Through Dandelion, who had known him previously (having purchased his biological son, Hello, on auction), I had been there for his meteoric self-piloted descent from celebrity to bookie, which profession he had always wanted to be in because of his passion for numbers. Unfortunately, that talent, combined with the piles of stewed prescience he consumed, made him the oddsmaker as well, and one who couldn't be beaten.

In any case my wife grew deficient by the day and hour as all of the little insights of life escaped her. Gambling, I believe, filled the vacancy. The Big Delicious was the axis of a cycle he didn't even know existed, as it wasn't an *event*, the context to which he was accustomed. Mannequins were born because of his gluttony. The Mannequin Ball came into being because a scalp net was installed in his skull. Money traded over the dummies he sucked of enlightenment. And then one day the Gamekeepers found Dandelion, shrunken to a pallid photogenic skeleton and they took her away to the Arena, for television consumption. The *glimmers* were there of course, but Hello snatched them out of their flight paths before the Big Delicious could burp from his previous meal. She went off to die riding hydrogen balloons in the Arena while she owed a small fortune to her bookmaker.

I think Hello wanted his adoptive mother to perish in competition. He has a sense of the aesthetic that is undeniable. The beauty of the Big Delicious being denied his monetary due on the day of his death is one of many examples. Hello and I have been close from the start, but our relationship is based upon *his* knowledge that *I* will not conform to societal strictures. It is why I put up with his mother when she grew pale from the exertion of being without kindling; it is why I continue to put up with him when he knows where I will have lunch even when I do not.

~

As we prepared for the worst, the candle flame still danced its defiant dance. I leaned that way but couldn't bring myself to blow it out. In spite of its wavering, it was constant, resilient. It lived when the life it represented did not. I let it burn, now low, almost in the icing, while Hello used a defense against our visitors that I could only ride the coattails of. They had added shouts to their poundings when I saw the charged *glimmer* pass through the door.

Beyond the door, a silence. Then a slow, elongated, unisonous gasp, in total contradiction to the definition of the term. The door stood like some primeval gateway suddenly showing the corrosion on its long-dutiful mechanisms. Behind it were the beings of another school of creation, smeared with the seepage from the Big D's burned out nostrils, the concept of a moment of greater understanding hanging like deposits from their bestial features. I found myself wondering, during that strange and wondrous interval, whether or not my beloved degenerate gambler had kept a concealed gun around the house.

An abrupt roar from one of the super-dimensional miscreants prefaced the door crashing down (which proved in a way that they had not been completely deprived of their sense of the future). Simultaneously, I had a déjà vu as powerful as I have ever had (which likewise proved that I had not been completely stripped of my sense of the past). I met my attacker with the only thing I had—the knife I should have been carving the cake with. At least I was still carving her memory as I slashed at Guido's descending arm, eliciting the equivalent of an operatic miscue. Something wasn't right as the white and blue cake appeared in the fray, the flame sucking out dully, just like the end, and Hello failing in his bid to launch his unlikely weapon as the sticky sugary shower drowned his adult-sized curses.

I swung the blade again, had it ripped out of my hand, saw the gleaming instant of my death, tasted icing, and was off to that Coral Mansion on…

~

Low.

I'd come home again, and all my wife's Mannequin Ball losses like so many daydreams in the Big D's fat-fingered hands.

"Seventy, eighty, ninety, TWELVE. There it is, you sweet boy! As soon as you pay the expenses for the injuries to Hugo's arm, we are square."

No, Big D—as the whole phosphorescent blob of him came into focus—*one of us is definitely not* square.

"Would you like a drink? A Coral Mansion cocktail heavy on the *vu*?"

"Where's Hello?"

"I can't keep up with that boy."

Yet I noticed something different about him, a surplus phosphorescence and bloatedness, a general overmuchness matched only by his inadvertent but quite obvious restraint. The *glimmers* spun around him like flies, and his flesh quivered with a musical regularity, but he wasn't *active* as he normally was. He had counted the money with the expected interest, but he hadn't *relished* it. He caressed it even now, but as if he were caressing the handle of a crutch.

I said, "There's no one you can't keep up with, Delicious. What have you done with him?"

He leaned forward, a great exercise: "I know what he tried to accomplish with my men, so I finished the deed for him, with my personal stamp. They still have not recovered from the shock of being no more." He closed one fatty eye in an effort at a wink. "I fed Hello thirteen *premos* and put him to bed. I figure if he doesn't wake up, the *glimmers* are necromancy."

"Wake him up."

"Ha. On whose command?"

"Your own. He predicted your death."

"Oh? And I can't do that myself?"

"Apparently this time, no."

"He also predicted the death of my men, but who had to make it happen."

"They're dead, aren't they?"

He laughed in jiggles and glints. "Touché."

"Where is he?" I said.

"Before we get into that, would you like to sniff some of my good stuff?" I followed his chunky finger to the tanks along the rough coral-surface wall. Lights overhead reflected on the bald heads, the *glimmers* like glitter on their rounded surfaces, bristling electromagnetically. The faces of the young men suspended in the water told of raptures unavailable on the street. If there was any toe on their opulent master's feet which they would not suck, it wasn't evident here.

"I amend my remark that there's no one you can't keep with," I told his opulence. "Sure, I'd love to show you how to sniff the good stuff."

"*Ho ho*," he blew. (Indeed, like Claus.) "Have you indulged in the more sublime pleasures before?"

"Dandelion turned me on to a taste of your—what's the word she used? Exotica? But the rest of us obviously don't have access to your boundless supply." I gestured luxuriantly.

"So Dandy was paying attention after all. Splendid! I could never get her to partake with me. Business and pleasure, I suppose."

I wanted to plunge my fingers in his eyes, but I imagined two black holes sucking all the *glimmers* in the universe into his unfathomable density. A belated chuckle from him made me wonder if he could follow my individual thoughts. Considering his magnificent appetite, his equally lavish arrogance, I decided that for my (tenuous) purposes it didn't matter.

"So let's get to it, Delicious. And do me a service—now that we're square and all—and refrain from referring to my late wife as Dandy."

"You drive a hard bargain, Zen, particularly when the dope's on me—but okay. Now take this and make a straw out of it." Not to my surprise, what dropped out of his engorged digits was one of the bills he had been caressing.

The action brought our persons closer than I'd have liked, even on a Sunday, and I heard a sigh, a great cumbersome sigh from his bulk. The *glimmers* humming around him like bees about the hive sparked in my eyelashes, on my breath. There was clearly something amiss here, and lo, but I was going to exploit it.

"So what is it I'm to do with a thousand spot, D?"

"Roll it up, you pagan," he said, sitting back on his slabs. "Let's *glitz.*"

Despite what I'd said, which I rather suspected he didn't believe to start with, I'd never done the thing I was about to do. Holding the rolled up note in my fingers, I tilted my head towards the nearest tank.

No sooner had he nodded in reply than a live picture of the Mannequin Ball appeared on the coral wall behind the receptacle, balloons bouncing across the court, their pale naked riders flailing and trying to keep a grip on the pommel all at the same time. For a moment I was mesmerized, seeing the rerun of Dandelion's aloha, so much gas out of the strange, funky sail of life and its caprices.

I shut out everything but the task at hand as I stepped over to the tank, leaned down and snorted every last *glimmer* off the poor college kid's scalp. A dozen images compounded by a syrup of *I swear I almost know where I came from and I want to go back!* spiced with a concoction of *Did I already take this picture?* succumbed to the superimposed face of Hello, surrounded by pillow, one comradely eye winking like I was on the right track and he'd known so all along. *Then* came the chemical responses, spinning around in me like little tornados, rendering my nerve endings the unlikely filaments that held the tossed salad in harmony.

"That's pretty good shit, Delish," I confessed. "But you really think you can keep up with *me*? Who do you think put the mannequin in Dandelion? Every déjà vu, every intuition, every premonition, every *spark* was mine after she turned me on."

For a second I saw that superfluous spark in the Big D's bulbs, but he wouldn't commit to the truth, even now that he was breathing in waves. I gestured he do his thing and waited to be dazzled on top of my dazzlement. The Big D did not disappoint. He snorted every *glimmer* off every head in the room, and then croaked in frustration when the scalp net itself did not suck off of the skull of his last slave subject. As he jerked his mass around to tell me about it, his eyes blazed with the spectacle of his mind. I asked him if he was sure he hadn't missed any.

"What's left?" he scintillated.

"Where's Hello?"

"Eh?"

"Hello's *glimmers* would be the icing on the,"—*Dandelion's*—"cake. Who but Hello attracts *glimmers* like you do? Are you intimidated your own son?"

"Where is that boy?" demanded the big Delicious.

"Where is he, Big D?"

Again came the unbidden image, Hello winking at me from some bed, somewhere.

"If you're unwilling to explore that avenue, I will. I fucking will, D. Where is he?"

He moved like the great movement that he was, calling doors open in advance of him, filling the air with his exhalations, squeezing what oxygen there was through his cellulite. "Hello," he murmured. Hello.

"I'm here, Delicious."

And there he was, at the end of the cul-de-sac in front of us, pillowed by coral walls, and the aura of him.

"Hello,"—the Big D's voice had a wheezing quality to it—"I want your *glimmers*. I'll return them with interest."

"Come and get them then," said Hello. And the air in the corridor, upon those words, began to ignite, particles accelerating through the scientists' super tubes.

"Gently, though," said the Big D, wavering like Dandelion's thirty-first flame. "I am only so much Delicious."

Only so much Delicious: a circumstance that belied the entire culture of him, his cult, his godhood. As I watched him huff and heave as he tried to ingest it all, even what wasn't there, I knew the game had been decided. He had overdosed.

There was a flushed departure of the *glimmers*, then a new honeycomb formed of the scattered cells, centering on a shiny point that might have been a lad's aesthetic eye.

Waltz With the Echoes

Part I:

POISON

On a drab gray morning in the heart of the Quarterthird, Konrad tapped on the door of his companion Ursula's laboratory and announced that he was going in search of his origins.

"Now?" she said through the wood, its oaken grain a familiar language to Konrad. He imagined her glancing up from her work with mild interest, then returning to the lens of a microscope as she offered, "You know the trains aren't running due to the storm. Where do you propose to locate your origins?"

"I thought I'd start in Trier, with the one who found me."

A brief silence, perhaps as she tinkered with the focus or adjusted the slide. "Laila merely discovered the babe washed up on shore. She did not see how you arrived there."

"Still, it is a starting point."

"Somehow, Konrad, I feel you are not telling me everything."

He sensed that her attention was now fully on the door. Conscious of the shape and heft of his words, he said, "She is a relic of the First Age. That is why you sent the boy Rein to her."

"The mystery to which Rein sought an answer *pertained* to the First Age."

He let the absence of words speak for him.

"Are you having dreams again, Konrad?"

He thought to point out that if she slept in the same bed with him she would know the answer to that question, but he would not bandy cruelty.

"I will be back by the end of the Quarterthird," he said.

A pause ensued, during which Konrad willed the door to open, for Ursula to throw herself into his arms. What he got was something equally as uncharacteristic: "When you return I want to share something with you."

Puzzled, he offered a quiet goodbye and turned away. Before he reached the end of the hall, the laboratory door opened behind him.

"I shall miss you," she said.

He did not turn, but as he hoisted his pack onto his back, he could almost feel her hands there helping with the straps. Touching him.

~

In the wake of the tingestorm the forest was a strange realm. The temperature had risen considerably since the two-day blizzard had dropped some fifty centimeters of snow, and the boughs of the fir trees now rained the melt in a symphony of stark echoes. Beyond the noises, a certain chromium gloom deepened with the forest's densities, rendering the lichen that draped copiously from the limbs an even grimmer shade of blue. As Konrad moved steadily through the trees, entrusting his balance and bearing to the spherial beneath his feet, the contrasts played off the questions he carried with him.

They were questions that had haunted him for much of his existence; indeed, could not be distinguished from the existential mysteries. *Who am I? Where did I come from? To what purpose do I walk this wasted Terra?* Until these past six years in Ursula's company, he had always had a diversion. In his youth he had drifted around the orphanage beneath the steadying hand of the serums they administered and the lies they wove. When they loosed the adult Konrad on the streets of Trier, he had found a sort of nightmarish solace in the substance *paradigm*. But when Ursula had rescued him from the new drug's clutches, literally pulling him up out of the gutter by his filthy hair, the sense of being without an identity at last caught up with him. Even then it took six years to come to terms with the abiding fear—fear of returning to paradigm, fear of losing Ursula, fear of what he would discover in his search—and finally commit to his course.

He had actually made his decision a few days before he informed Ursula. As if in response to that decision, the worst tingestorm in a half decade had come out of nowhere, burying the world and its mysteries in silver-flecked white, shutting down longer distance travel except by river. Had he waited another week or two, conditions would likely have proven far more favorable for such a journey, but he had not graven his commitment in stone only to see it subjected to the erosion of time *and* weather.

The river was Konrad's immediate destination. In Mystischshatten he would be able to buy passage to Reliquien and hopefully beyond to Totenheim, where the Mystisch River flowed into the Rhein. One could travel all the way to Trier by boat, as the ancient city was located on the Mosel River, which emptied into the Rhein at ruined Koblenz some two hundred kilometers north of Totenheim. It was a journey Konrad had taken before—in the company of Ursula, who had no interest in trains. "Look!" she'd announced as the *Deutsches Eck* and its fallen statue of the mounted Kaiser Wilhelm had come into view. "*There* is an artifact that belongs in the Trier's' Reliquary." Though there would be many more as they entered the Rhein Gorge with its majestic castle ruins perched high over the river, none meant more to her than the Wilhelm, which stood as a symbol of "unity," a concept the world of the Third Age, "sorely lacked."

He was not looking forward to following that same route and its memories. Better a thousand times that the storm had never come and he had been able to journey at least a portion of the way by train. For he had still been the paradigm's slave when traveling with Ursula, and save for the rare moments of clarity that she had seemed to impose upon him by her own will, the trip had been a feverish, delirious agony of sleeplessness and spasms, endless thirst and visions. He had visited the drug once since that time, and always kept two cubes on his person for insurance; he hoped these connections to the nightmare served as a deterrent rather than an anti-venom. He hoped for many things, not least a swift passage through these seemingly haunted woods.

Alas, the nature of the spherial was such that speed took a backseat to convenience. While there was an elegant ease to its motion, the sphere could not, by definition, exceed its function, which was to comfortably transport a person from point a to point b. Thus Konrad was at his vehicle's disposal as he made his way down the densely wooded mountain toward the river. Thoughts of Ursula accompanied him, but they took a backseat to *his* purpose, which was to know himself before he grew old and died. In this regard the wood, the trees reflected the moments of his life, gathering around him mysteriously, allowing only vague glimpses of what lay behind.

This seemed to be corroborated by an unexpected disturbance within the forest's acoustic chambers—a disturbance both aural and psychic in quality.

For at its first sounds Konrad felt a change visit him, a hollow, groundless yearning sensation…as if some desolate place inside him had been suddenly uncovered. He scanned his surroundings, looking for nostalgia among the weeping lichen and snow, the layered, murky moments of his life, but gleaned no impressions that seemed in any way connected to the overwhelming sense of…vacancy.

The noise increased as the source grew nearer, gradually revealing itself to the ears as a discordant symphony of honking, squawking, rattling and hooting; whistling, whining, whooping and warbling. The well inside Konrad swiftly filled with curiosity as he wondered what manner of madness his eyes were about to behold. He exerted pressure on the spherial through the ball of his right foot and came to a halt in the silvery half-light of the wood. Even had he wanted to avoid the disturbance by skirting its radius, he would have been powerless to do so. Such was the fascination that had replaced the void.

Then the thing emerged from out of the folds, and Konrad could only gape at its utter strangeness.

It might have been a single entity with various appendages, so fluid was its chaos, so rhythmic its discord. Yet that was the easy road for the senses, which sought to untangle the thing even as they dismissed it, to reject it even as they savored it through dissection. When the eyes and the ears and the subtler senses all came together with their impressions, the complex nature of the thing began to come forth, its members and tentacles to become life forms of their own.

Out of the circus emerged a circus, a traveling band of creatures mostly of a sort Konrad had never encountered, though his experiences had taken him through the preserves of both Trier and Reliquien as well as the dazzle-scape of paradigm.

The leader of the troupe was a bald sort with painted eyes and a multiplicity of necklaces hanging on his bare chest. Surrounding him were a cast of beasts and birds that tested human description, indeed spat in the face of it as they huddled around the call of their ringmaster's rattle. Luckily Konrad had absorbed what Ursula had taught him in the way of historical zoology and grasped—at whatever level—much of what he was looking at.

At the head of the company went what he perceived to be a Greek-myth marriage of South American and Middle Eastern origins, a parrot's head upon the body of an oversized Persian cat, licking its fur incessantly and coughing up endless fur balls on its thick black tongue. Behind the hybrid came the beast that actually pulled the wagon on which the leader and two other creatures sat. This beast had magnificent, wind-pushing ears that seemed to aid in the company's passage as readily as the animal's obvious power. In front of its ominous bulk swayed two great trunks, one clutching a tall wooden cross painted flame orange, the other a small uprooted tree with the suggestion of fruit still clinging to its twisted branches. The earthquake ensuing the beast's lumbering movements caused the creatures flanking the ringmaster to titter ceaselessly, an action amplified by every crack of the red whip the man wielded in the fist that did not hold the rattle. Both creatures were winged and feathered, the one with a beak that blathered in every tongue and tune—to match its body's every tone and texture—the other possessing a hideous unknown head with six bulbous eyes and hair growing out of its open mouth on the current of its contributory capitulations. On top of the latter's shiny metal cap perched an owl—the only creature among the company that Konrad had ever seen before—looking brightly around, occasionally contributing a single hooting note to the choir.

The wagon's bed was stacked high with its load, which writhed and struggled against the tarp secured over it. Now and then a flash of pale would appear between two of the tie-downs, yet only for a moment before being sucked back into the enclosure's roiling contents. Konrad could not imagine what form the squirmers took, though they were apparently many and feeble within their prison, high-pitched pleas mostly drowned out by the rest of the traveling chorus. The chord of panic that came through advised him that he would not want to be in the way when the tarp was snatched off and the load set free.

Completing the party, rolling behind the wagon inside a transparent globe partially filled with water, was what Konrad recognized as a seal, but one with its own distinctive features—most prominently, the two heads protruding happily out of the flippered lump of its body. On each of its noses balanced a bottle whose contents resembled the fluid that splashed against its glacier-blue fur as the seal led its big plastic ball along, though Konrad suspected something altogether less innocuous than mere water.

"*Poison!*" announced the leader of the troupe. "You there, sir! Look around you and tell me what you see!"

Konrad felt his left foot, of its own volition, begin to exert pressure on the spherial, but he commanded it to hover a moment or two while he assessed. He did not look around him as instructed, but rather kept his eye on the ringmaster as the latter stood in his seat, raising his rattle high and shaking it emphatically for a few seconds before letting it come to rest in a poised state above his head. The entire company and chorus, including its clandestine cargo, came to a standstill—which action seemed to echo through the forest.

"Go on, don't let your ancestors color your vision," said the conductor above his similarly poised orchestra. "Don't fear karmic retribution. Don't let the ghosts dissuade you. Tell me what do you see."

Konrad shook his head. "Dissuade me how?"

"From addressing the truth! *Poison! That* is what we are surrounded by. The work of our ancestors."

"This is some secret?" Konrad said.

"The truth is always secret," laughed the man. "That is its core nature." He shook his rattle again, a single movement, bringing a squeal from either the wagon bed or the ball behind it—Konrad could not tell which. Then the man lifted symbols from among the chains around his neck. "This Egyptian ankh. This Western crucifix. This Hebrew star. These speak to truth, each in its way. Will you?"

From out of images that abided at the hems of consciousness, Konrad said, quietly: "You...whoever you are...cannot imagine the truth."

"No, *you* cannot imagine the truth. What are you, with your special hindsight, but a historian? You must participate in events to truly understand their complexities. Look around you with the eyes in your head and describe to me what you see."

At last Konrad removed his gaze from the ringmaster. The gloom had deepened to a liquid state around them, receding from the feet of those who trod the forest floor, were apparitions in its midst. The forest itself, in all its ancient majesty, merely wept.

—*Like Jesus*, came a voice from among the silhouettes. Konrad momentarily found the strangely lucid gaze of the beast that transported the circus, its flame orange beacon suspended in time along with everything else—

Yet the forest's grief was also elusory: droplets at the tips of fingers of lichen, of boughs weighted to grotesquery by nature's white and endless vomit. Konrad looked around him and he saw despair; he saw the world into which he had been born.

"What do you want?" he said of the asker.

"I want you to say the word, sir, so that we can give you what you need and be on our way. It may not roll simply off the tongue, but it is the simplest of words. What my little menagerie carries is a cure for it. Who has not sought such? Who has not sought to be free of the restrictions of our environment?"

"I do not feel particularly threatened by our environment," said Konrad, "and so am not interested."

"Odd, I'd rather have suspected otherwise." He shook his rattle, again only once. Peepings sounded from under the hood. A continued stare from the beast that paused from its duty as mule. A *phuff phluff* from the feathery, multi-eyed creature to the ringmaster's left as he now stepped past it, hopping down from the wagon and approaching the seal toy in the rear.

"Yes, my dears," he said, opening a small window in the globe. The two heads appeared to vie for the honor before one successfully delivered the bottle it balanced to the ringmaster. In exchange he kissed it on the nose, then let the window closed again, turning toward Konrad. As he approached, Konrad repeated that he was not interested…through fragments of film, of holoplays that he did not want to be witness to.

"Don't fear," said the ringmaster. "This is water from the First Age, little more."

"I don't want it."

"Of course you do." He paused in his approach to bend down and retrieve a handful of glittering snow. To Konrad's bewilderment he took a bite out of the lump, proclaiming from amid the flecks: "It is a total cure. The bottle's contents render one completely and wholly immune." He swallowed demonstratively to punctuate his claim.

"I don't want it," said Konrad. And turned away from the ringmaster and his menagerie.

"You are *embedded* in the poison!" hissed the latter. "Certainly you shall have it!"

Though he sensed the tongues of darkness unfurling behind him, Konrad failed to react in time as the shadow overtook him, forcing the snow, not the bottle, upon him. He struggled vigorously but against the darkness was ineffectual. As he ingested the material, crystal by melting crystal, so did the dusk devour the troupe that had traveled into its subtle embrace, leaving only the cross staring back out of the silver dark, that and the fruits of the uprooted tree like the beast's sorrowful eyes.

Konrad stumbled away into the layers, uncertain of what had just happened to him. As he groped his way through the dripping trees toward the bottom of the hill, he heard in the distance the low, familiar grumbling of thunder, some comfort in the tinged and aethereal night. As the view of Mystischshatten opened before him, the scatter of lights along the river formed a negative of the season itself.

Which never ended.

Part II:
DELIRIUM

At a surly shack along the still ice-encrusted moorings, Konrad found a grounded salt on his fourth beer. A frothy contribution from Konrad revealed that the grizzled fellow skippered a small barge that had delivered a load of equipment to Teufelbronn upriver and now carried rare Mystisch wine for K´ln. The captain had lost his two crewmen to the tingestorm—a circumstance about which he volunteered no details, nor was asked for any—and needed at least one good man to hose down the decks, battle any additional weather, and make sure the ties remained fast for the journey to K´ln.

Konrad didn't need to convince the captain that he was the man. Obviously they'd mutual interests. Indeed, a continuous nonstop journey to the Mosel River was more than Konrad could have anticipated. They might be weighed in Totenheim or Franken, but he doubted so in these conditions. A spillway here or there would be the only delays, so they might well reach Koblenz within eight hours of departure, which the skipper informed him would be at sunrise now that the weather had begun to let up. As it happened *Der Schwan* had exactly two rooms, the one not occupied by the captain being predictably free. Konrad paid the sleepy-eyed barmaid/proprietress twice over for being open to business after such a storm.

As he ascended the stairs she inquired behind him, somewhat embarrassedly, "Is there anything I can get you...you know..."

He thought at first she was offering sexual companionship—a strange, indeed surreal proposal to his senses—but then he observed the hesitant movement of her hand, fingers grazing the skin below her right eye.

Touching his own cheekbone, he felt moistness, and a slight pain rising through the padding of the two beers he'd consumed. "No thank you," he told her with what he could muster in the way of a smile.

He could see that his refusal bothered her as he continued up the stairs. It didn't occur to him until he was inside his cubicle how lonely she seemed. It was only then, too, that he let himself think about how attractive she was, with her soft blue eyes and mussed hair and blouse. In the mirror opposite the short bed, he examined the place she had referred to and discovered, to his relief, merely the salty desert of unconscious tears.

Disrobing and crawling under the covers, acquainting himself with the withered pillows and mattress, he heard in the cabin next door two voices, and eventually the noises of passion. In the feeble light that infiltrated the room through the cracks between door and frame he fancied he could make out the motions of two silhouettes in the mirror as his hand began to wander and he remembered, for the first time in a long while, someone other than Ursula.

Afterwards, in the renewed darkness, Konrad could not sleep. The sense of release degraded to a feeling of uncleanliness and then the sort of panicked guilt associated with coming off a paradigm binge. His hands were clammy, his ankles sweated among the bunched covers he had kicked off his body, his cock lay shriveled and cold in the puddle of its own spend. The room around him, now utterly dark, felt like ice. As he sat up staring at the black mirror a bead of sweat rolled down across his face, and suddenly the panicked guilt transmogrified into something infinitely worse.

No! he chided himself. *A mere handful of tinged snow could not produce such results. Nausea maybe…perhaps a slight fever…*

He got up and turned on the light, examined his face again in the mirror, the skin of his arms, his moist naked chest. As his search revealed nothing, he allowed himself a moment of relief.

It's a paradigm attack, nothing more, brought on by that business on the hillside, the seed that zealot planted. Any other symptoms are psychosomatic.

He stared at himself, nodding, hearing words from a distant half-buried place, a place of children and those who molded and shaped them.

Thanks to time and medicine, we are largely immune now. To contract full-blown Fever, one's exposure to the tinge usually has to be both direct and prolonged as in a fleckstorm. Of course…

"'There are exceptions,'" he quoted aloud. And then couldn't look anymore as another drop of sweat ran down his neck over his clavicle. Sighting his pack resting along the wall, he realized just how badly he could use a paradigm cube.

He stood there for several seconds contemplating the prospect before a violent shiver overcame him and he succumbed.

Reaching among his clothes for the pouch sewn inside the pack's lining, his hand discovered something unexpected. A fresh thrill coursed his nervous system as he brought out the object, knowing before putting his eyes on it what it was. His jaw nonetheless hung slack as he stared at the bottle that had mere hours ago been bobbing on a seal's snout.

The zealot had obviously put it in Konrad's bag during the struggle. Had that been the whole purpose of the attack?

You are embedded *in the poison! Certainly you shall have it!*

Why the snow then? To prove the point? Why any of it? Today people lived and died of other causes. Scar tissue had formed of inhaling four thousand years of the end of the world. He reached in the bag again, finding the small phial containing the paradigm cubes. He weighed the respective bottles in his hands.

Four thousand years, Ursula?

Four thousand years of Darkness, Konrad. Four millennia spanning the violent end of the First Age and the mysterious awakening into the Third. That awakening occurred a mere three and a half centuries ago. In many ways we must still consider ourselves part of the Dark Age. They won't be erecting statues of the like of Kaiser Wilhelm anytime soon.

He found the larger bottle to be a much better fit in his hand as he let his fingers explore the glass containers. His mind wandered back to the streets of Trier, where she had looked down on him in the gutter, citing her name as if it were the universe.

Where did you come from, Ur-su-la?

"They say that I came from the Dark Age. Indeed my mum once mused that I was born out of chromosomes and time, twin sisters in a pagan eternity. Get up, you Edgar Allan Poe. Get up and come home with me."

Edgar who?...There is strong geological evidence that intelligent life did not exist on this continent during the Dark Age ...Do you have any paradigm at your home?

He paced the small room, bottles tottering on his palms as they had on the noses of the seals, though in this case containing two separate substances. The more he reflected, the less a comparison there seemed between the "water from the First Age, little else" cure and the paradigm. Eventually he opened the bottle in his right hand, emptying out a single cube into his palm. It was then he caught sight of himself in the mirror again, gasping.

His face and upper body were spotted in red swellings.

With trembling hands he returned the cube to its keep, then opened the bottle that had stowed away in his pack, drinking down its contents and tossing the empty container aside. Turning off the light, he smothered himself in the pillows, unwilling to be distracted by anything that did not resemble oblivion…should his old companion prove kind enough to rear its worthy head before dawn.

~

As the Rhein flowed darkly before them toward its distant date with the Ice North Sea, Konrad considered his own rendezvous with unknown waters. That the river's origins were behind them while his own, hopefully, were in front of them did not weaken the comparison. Indeed a poetic irony arose out of the notion that the current of his existence flowed *against* gravity even as his flesh succumbed to it. His life had never known a fluid course, nor had it followed the path of least resistance—sometimes by choice, more often by external forces. Since washing up on the banks of the Mosel River as a child, he had been at the mercy of randomness and disorder (*entropy*, one of Ursula's esoteric terms, surfaced).

At the orphanage they had blatantly lied to him about when he had been discovered and how he had come to be orphaned. He had learned such while still in the facility's care—long before Ursula, with her eerie knowledge of things, had rescued him from the streets of Trier. Her acquaintance with his discoverer, that same revenant whom he was now on his way to see, had merely supported what he had found out by placing his ear to the vents. He had not been a four-year-old shipwreck survivor, but an infant of unknown origins. Perhaps even more strange than his appearance on the river banks was the dark hole in his memory preceding age four. He understood that some people did not remember so far into their pasts, but his own recollections were very clear back to that starting point, when he had been shown around the orphanage, his new home, *as though* he had just come into the institute's keeping. Before that, blackness. His own Dark Age of four millennia…in years.

Konrad had been tempted to blame the gap in his memory on trauma to do with the headmaster. A psychology existed there, to be certain; however, the sometimes passing, sometimes bold explorations of the administrator's hands remained all too clear in Konrad's mind—unsuppressed moments in time glowing angrily and sharply as the red swellings that covered his body. In a way the behavior of the headmaster had been a constant among the randomness and disorder, even while validating it.

Another had been the drugs, administered in cyclical precision in what the cleanwhites termed the "Nietzschean solution" (later Ursula had been able to shed some light on this, describing the First Age philosopher's concept of a Superman). "To prevail," the one administering the serum would sometimes utter. Konrad knew now that this proclamation had referred to mankind in general. He knew now that the drugs were genetic enhancers. He knew now that the often irrational, sometimes fatal behavior of his fellow orphans was the sacrifice toward enduring the mistakes of man. He knew many things, and yet so little in the end, a victim of chaotic inevitability in a laboratory environment.

The victim and his lot took wings from there unhampered, soaring out of the facility of the abandoned into a city of the abandoned, which proved equally kind in its ministrations. The streets of Trier, as they unfurled before him, possessed a deceptive allure, easily obscuring their potential to further the cause of the victim. Willpower and responsibility were involved in surrendering oneself to the city; something more than that as one stood beneath the mighty Roman artifact of the Porta Nigra, gateway to the inner city and beyond, and avowed to finally know some kind of existence. Decision making was required to succumb to the dark curvaceous women that gathered among the gate's sentry paths, beckoning, tossing down flower petals on the court as if to birth palaces. A goodbye kiss to the soul as one placed the coin in the doorkeeper's hand and ascended into the strange vaults of blackened stone.

Indeed Trier might have existed to further the cause of the victim, to create a subject that even an Ursula might want. A whisper of meaninglessness that a Dark Age relic might share journeys with, not only then but later, as randomness and disorder struck in every season, with a fleckstorm-like suddenness and impact. A question that a Practitioner might deign to answer, if only she could...

Now that the Fever had manifested itself, he might never find answers. The captain had been gracious enough not to mention the marks on his face, but the various senseless duties he had been put to since departure made it evident that the grizzled fellow was quarantining him in a fashion—even though no intelligent person really believed the sickness was contagious. Konrad could not complain, however. He had wondered, while looking at his naked body in the mirror before descending the stairs at *Der Schwan*, just how far he would get in his condition. The proprietress, to her credit, had not let disgust or embarrassment hinder her from collecting. If the captain had seriously pondered denying him access to the *Eimer voller Wein*, his steely-cold survivor of a barge, it hadn't shown over his steaming coffee.

The sentiment was nonetheless there, in the gestures if nowhere else, as the weathered captain piloted the vessel like some skeleton about the mist. Words fell off him like flesh, the day fled before him like memory, the fog submitted to his otherworldly presence. The road became one of complements, reminiscent of the Ursula voyage, an aching sense of detachment to accent the dreadful beauty of the surroundings. Cliffs rose in splendid constancy, traces of vines spilling over their brows, reminding Konrad of things he'd seen only in dreams. He echoed some of these thoughts at the skipper, who ignored him at the helm. His skin hurt from being stretched by its eruptions, his lips and brow, his tongue, his fingers felt hot. He retired below decks to his cabin, but it was an action, nothing more. He'd no purpose and no desire, except perhaps for water...

Which brought him to a well. To his satisfaction, not only was the well in working order, but a primitive pulley served a rope down into the blackness of the shaft—which, upon the drop of a stone, proved at least ten meters deep.

Enough to lose three hags in.

Above, he heard the captain, as if in synchronization with his thoughts, call, "Hail, City of Relics."

Which meant Reliquien and its grand *Schloss* ruin, another surviving treasure of the First Age, had come into sight. Konrad's mind and senses spun with the memories—the wretched threesome that had kidnapped Ursula and brought her into the hands of the Sire of Reliquien, his own journey to the castle to rescue her. It was in that bizarre interim that he had come upon Rein, whom Ursula would eventually send to the Revenant Laila for help in translating an ancient document that had somehow arrived in the boy's hands. Rein and his purpose had visited Konrad since these events took place (only the Quarterfirst of last year?) and would again, he knew. For that was the way and the wont of the world—as he fell on the cot, feeling flush.

And of ancient sheepskin parchments—as he wiped the sweat from his brow with the back of his hand, smacked his mouth dryly.

Strange messages from antiquity—as he reached behind him to the water tank, pouring from the tap into his hand, then salvaging whatever he could with his swollen tongue.

The markings had been even more exotic than the material, like the marks on papyruses, caves walls, on doors. Like firstborn sons out of books. Like babes in bulrushes. What had he called himself, that ringleader of a cross-bearing circus? Why had these images struck a chord with Konrad? Who was he with the puss weeping from his sores?

Like Jesus.

Am I the same, that prophet off Ursula's lips, that Buddha in the kiss she never shared with me, that Allah and God Which is a paradox in that It cannot forge a weapon too mighty for It to wield? Am I the cold pall that has covered this Terra since before Ursula rose from the debris and walked upright? The living manifestation of all of these? Am I the lost soul of the planet?

"Konrad!" came the captain's voice through the fever. "Up on deck, you. They will want to know that I have a man as we pass through."

Indeed? Is that too of existential quality?

The standing, the strange standing was what it was and more as he leaned on that crutch they had given him, that secret knowledge that the orphan had a genetic edge over all the other children. And just perhaps, as he made his way up to the deck and hung on the bulwark looking up at the men armed with both weapons and scopes, he had been brought from below to show off his sores, lest they be tempted to delay the captain on his great mission. While Konrad had no idea how even rare wine gave the captain such privilege, he did appreciate his own rareness in the matter, opening his shirt that there be no mistake as to his condition. When the captain told him that wasn't necessary, he laughed at him: "Isn't it, skipper?"

"You are drunk with fever. Don't die on my boat. I wouldn't know what to do with you."

"I don't have a name. Toss me in the river."

"That, I might."

Konrad laughed at him, and at the guards above them as they passed beneath the bridge. In the end this was his journey and they were the props. To punctuate this fact for the lot of them he traipsed back to the stern and began untying two of the ropes that kept the heavy canvas over the load, intending to place his boot on one of the barrels in a pose. That's when things ceased being what they had been and his blood, over the remonstrations of the skipper, cried for paradigm.

For as the hitches were liberated the cargo began to move, to writhe beneath the tarp. He stood there with a rope in each fist, gaping as the pale host, a thousand bristling spiders, scurried from under the hems of the canvas, along the ropes, his arms, and into the white noise of remembrance. Places and times that had never, even in the profoundest grip of paradigm, been his own. And yet smothered him like the pall of snow.

~

Among the white, Konrad saw a cold room full of heated argument. He watched the one who presided there put down the often vehement protests of the room's occupants again and again. The language seemed familiar to him and yet he could not translate the words, only the actions—which clearly centered on a figure separated from the proceedings by a wall, and armed men. This person remained in shadow until the dissent in the adjoining room reach an explosive pitch; then he emerged from the shade just long enough to show Konrad his bald head, his painted eyes and draping necklaces, the phial in his hand. Then withdrew, like breath.

A feeling touched Konrad, an instinct, and he knew it was not just his, but that of humanity as a whole. Though it lacked the naked urgency of foreboding, it possessed the subtler elements that made it all the more real to those who, from all corners of the world, experienced it. The knowledge and visions swept before Konrad like the unfurling tapestry of time, a holoplay of a gargantuan fleckstorm in the making. He saw Mankind gather its wits, its artifacts, its data at the prospect of what was to come. He saw it apply its contingencies even as the seasons endured—withstanding, as it always had, the fighting of nations, the dissolving of alliances, the forging of new weapons. He saw people at the individual level act upon the sense of teetering at the edge of oblivion by boarding ships and trains for safer latitudes, looking for shelter from their fears, their expectations, their *knowledge* of the end.

He saw a single train car surrounded by snow. Faces of various types occupied the car: the anxious, the disturbed, the overwrought, the hopeless; yet all sharing the common thread of disquiet. He watched a boy with strange blue hair pass out scrolls to the car's passengers. *Do not fear*, the boy told them. *There will be a new beginning. These conflicts of your world will very soon be a thing of the past. Absorb these written words I offer you. Your eyes will not recognize them, nor your conscious mind be able to interpret their message, but the older part of you, the part that lived before your Terran existence, will understand.*

He saw the boy raise fiery green eyes to look at him, then place a finger on his lips, shushing the orchestrations of memory.

Or was that the whispers of the thick layer of storms descending on the world...

Part III:

PANACEA

He woke to a chill. Motion. Mist clinging to what he instantly recognized as the slopes of the Mosel River valley. Patches of vineyards appeared intermittently, as did stark bluffs, suggestions of forest. He tasted the scent of the river on his tongue as he began to sit up and was gently pushed back. Out of the mist a pair of eyes emerged, sudden because of their brilliant emerald color, unsettling because of their frank, naked gaze.

"You!" said Konrad. "I have seen you before. Who are you?"

"I am the Lord of Cochem Castle and captain of this vessel," he said, tilting his head slightly, bringing his young features momentarily into view.

"I saw…"

"I know, but it doesn't matter now. You are resting from the poison. Silence is best as you recover and I navigate us through the fog."

"But you are only a boy," Konrad said.

The face smiled, but issued no words.

"Do you have a name to go along with your title?"

"Aen."

"Cochem Castle…that is the one between Koblenz and Bernkastel." Ursula had made sure that he look upon its amazing intactness and grandeur even through his paradigm fever. "How did you become lord of a castle? I thought most of the ruins along the Mosel belonged to the Trier Reliquary."

"Shh." That finger on the lips, those sudden eyes. "You are not just disturbing the mist; you are disturbing your own healing. Perhaps you would do better below decks, where the temptation to speak is not so great."

While he felt a stranger to his own circumstance, Konrad recognized wisdom, age in the youth's words. A hundred questions brimmed, but he refrained from speaking them. As the silence crystallized among the condensed air, Aen withdrew to the helm, located somewhere behind Konrad's makeshift bed. He tried to observe the boy at the post, but the strain on his neck was too much and he opted instead for the valley's slopes, which seemed far too high and insensitive to acknowledge an infant washed up at their feet. The thought to try the quietude by querying his strange guide on that count occurred to him, but he realized he was too tired to bother.

He was almost asleep when he felt a blanket being placed over him. The fragrance of the vineyards swaddled him.

~

Who am I?

Shouldn't you ask, who are we?

Who are you?

I am Aen. I am of no consequence. I am content.

But what do you know of me?

Of you? I know that you are another beginning. Another and another and another. Do you remember what I told you on the train to obscurity?

Not me—the passengers.

We are all passengers.

What did you say?

I said: As you whisper farewell to your small personal lives, fear not for humanity as a whole. For out of the ashes of this age will come new ages, new beginnings, new pursuits.

Is that what the scroll said?

The scroll speaks in an ancient language. Do you remember that language?

The characters seemed familiar to me.

Seemed?

I saw the parchment that Rein carried.

Saw?

The characters are there…I can just make them out.

It doesn't matter. Yours is a new language. Man's is a new language.

What does that mean?

Surely you are too obsessed with your own paths to be interested in those of your species.

Is there a difference?

That is astute of you, and another indication that you are coming out of your fever. The marks on your body are evaporating. Your eyes grow more clear. I can now hear you when you think. I hear the bell of your soul. Still, silence is a much more glorious place. It is the tide with the moon. Or have you forgotten that too? Night's Roman token?

The partial Roman coin hung utterly, and magnificently, against the drape of night as Konrad emerged from below. The captain was at the wheel, old, somehow older than he had been, though he still wore a boy's clothes.

"Man," Aen said, nodding to a seat along the bulwark, "survived the First Age apocalypse because he is that sort of willful, resilient, and perseverant animal. Ingenuity played a part in it. So did desperation. So did instinct. So, also, did history. For such has always been his response in dire times. Memory guides him. And not only the sort contained in books and on film and chips, but a deeper memory, a genetic memory, a psychic memory. It has even been set forth that he remembers his future. That his moments in time are blueprints in the same way as his DNA—"

"Excuse me. Set forth by whom?"

"Theorists," said Aen, emeralds intensifying for a moment. "Of course said memory seems to serve him only when his need is greatest. His mistakes happen with entropic inevitability,"—*to use one of Ursula's terms*—"the latter days of the First Age being the macrocosm of that unfortunate reality. In the face of a war featuring weapons that had mere decades before not even been conceived of, man laid before him two paths, one towards escaping his follies, the other towards enduring them. Both found their origins here in Europa, where the conflict was centered and where the political,"—*to use another*—"environment was at its most unstable."

"Yes, I saw a room, and men making decisions. I saw…"

Again Aen's eyes ignited, as though he were privy to awesome secrets. "The first of these paths took the form of an airship that would contain not just human beings, but man's great artistic treasures as well, which expressions, it was decided, best represented man's identity, his being, his soul (indeed, Konrad, you should perhaps look at your own creations in your search). This ship left the planet but days before the weapons that would destroy civilization—and render almost all life on Terra extinct—were utilized."

With wonder Konrad watched him tend the wheel, peer out into the mist, open such gates into the Dark Age of mankind. "But where did they go? What became of them?"

"In time they found a habitable world. They endured there, as humans do, but not in the way that they have endured here. For humans are also adaptable; on Aegea, as they named the watery planet, they were forced to be. Indeed, the colonizers' integration with their planet provided a blueprint—or perhaps *im*print is the better word, as this transfer occurred solely through the obscure intricacies of human wiring—for our own survival on Terra. 'Our,' say I. Isn't it lovely that I am so inclusive?

"The second path was forged in Scandinavia to the north of us. Whereas technology carved the way for the former, science did the latter, involving genetic enhancement as a means of surviving the fallout sure to ensue the use of the weaponry at hand. Discoveries that would have moved the world prior to the cataclysm were kept under hat—and in continual development—until such time as their application translated to breath itself. Then no one cared. For all man's tinkering, God Himself had lost interest. Do you know God, Konrad?"

Startled, Konrad answered, "Why are you asking?"

"Because you met him along the road, did you not, in the guise of a ringmaster?"

"What do you know of it?"

"I know he fed you not the cure for your fever, but the fever itself. Are you so blind?"

Konrad could but stare at him, echoing, "God…"

"Wasn't it Him, then, Undoer of Creation?"

Konrad revisited the scene, the words, the struggle, the phial pushed on him, "I don't know who or what he was…"

"Don't you?"

"Has he something to do with my identity?" *My being. My soul.*

"Peripherally, one might say. As you, Konrad, are part of Humankind's third path."

Konrad's gaze wandered to the smear of the gibbous moon beyond the mist. "You said man followed but two paths."

"I did."

"How is it possible then that I'm part of a third?"

"That is the question indeed."

"What is the third path's nature?"

"Look! The mist parts before us. What is that city ahead?"

As the structures rose on both banks, the word needn't be spoken. They both recognized ancient Trier, greatest of all First Age artifacts. Konrad turned back to the skipper, with wants, with questions, but Aen receded and would converse no more except to say that his own part was now almost done.

"Do you mean for now? Forever? Who are you?"

I? Ask Carmen. Maybe she knows. The revenant knows me better than anyone.

~

When the Basilica's massive doors parted and she stood there before him, Konrad found himself momentarily at a loss for words. It wasn't her youthful elegance as a light breeze stole in from outside, touching at her simple indigo gown, her long honey-colored hair; nor the unnatural paleness exhibited in her otherwise lovely face, her bare arms and feet; nor even the frosted blue eyes that seemed to measure him from out of a wasteland. He was struck at a deeper, more personal level.

"I know you," he managed at last.

A vague smile came to her features. "I tend to have that effect on people. It is why they refer to me as the revenant."

"You? I was expecting someone…"

"More oracular? A wise old ghost? I am still that." She invited him in with a gesture of her hand.

As he moved past her into the vast hall, she suddenly stepped back, expression changing. "I sense *him* about you. Where have you been?"

"I-I'm not sure…"

She recovered quickly, "I'm sorry. Never mind me. How are you?"

"Do you remember me?"

"How could I forget our child of the vineyards?"

His eyes narrowed. "Don't call me that."

She met his gaze across the scathed terrain. "Yes…I should have known better. Have you been back to the orphanage?"

He faced the interior of the Basilica. "My memories of the orphanage are not fond ones."

She said nothing as she closed the doors.

The open cavernous spaces were rendered less so by heavy black curtains hanging over both levels of tall arched windows. He couldn't help but stare at the long vertical drapes as the revenant led him to the center of the nave, where lamps suspending from the lofty ceiling cast a thin glow over an out of place assortment of wooden furniture, the only objects between the building's entrance and the semi-circular apse at the far end.

"The tinge-aether, all the whiteness out there, disturbs me," she said, motioning to a chair.

As he took the offered seat he wondered on what terms she was with the gloom. Indeed, what did she do in this place, dwarfed by its hollow immensity? Waltz with the echoes?

She sat opposite him. "Believe it or not, I knew nothing of what went on inside the orphanage during my thirty-three years of transporting children there. Until I became corporeal again, I knew only my function. But that is not why you are here."

"No. I am here because I am seeking my origins."

"I should have expected you long before now."

"Do you have any knowledge of my identity?"

"No." She watched him with eyes more gray than blue in the limited glow.

"You are a relic of the First Age, Laila."

"I am Carmen now. This DNA-bred body was more than a gift to me." Her expression changed slightly. "Ah, forgive me, Ursula has not told you my story."

"Ursula does not tell me much. But I know some of your story. You were on a train at the end of the world. You are a relic of the First Age, Carmen."

"So I am. I'm tempted to ask how that relates to your situation, but I suspect you would not be here on a whim."

He leaned forward, that the momentousness of the subject not be sucked away into the emptiness surrounding them. "Ursula sent Rein to you with his parchment because you were there, at the end of the world." He tapped his chest. "I. I was there. I have seen such terrible things, Carmen."

"I sense that you have, Konrad," she said. "But not because you were there.

Your visions are of a different source."

"What source?" Konrad said.

"I do not know. I can think of only one who might be able to answer that question. Alas, he comes and goes as he chooses."

"Is his name Aen?"

In surprise: "Yes. Do you know him?"

"Do *you*, Carmen? You, he said, know him better than anyone."

A soft smile came then went. "He said that, did he? I fear no one really knows Aen."

"He gave you a scroll. You know its meaning."

"I do. But again, pertinence."

"Look in my eyes and tell me you do not believe it has something to do with me."

She sighed. "Other than Aen, there are but two individuals on this Terra who know what that document contains. You would be the third? How can I trust that you are not *his* thing? You reek of him, Konrad. Like you reek of years of paradigm."

"He? *He?* Of whom do you continue to speak?"

She observed him for some seconds, weighing, measuring. At last she said:

"The Balkan Lucien Kovic. Like myself, he is a remnant of the First Age. It was his actions that set into motion the events that led to the end of civilization."

"What actions?"

"He raped and murdered children."

"And I know this fiend?"

"He is elusive. He sabotages with drugs and words."

Oh no.

"He is Satan, and Iblis, and all of that and more. He prowls the world seeking what he has not yet destroyed."

Konrad looked around him at the black curtains, the vastness of his keep. "I have nothing to do with him. What of the document and its message? What of me? What of the four lost years previous to my first memories of the orphanage?"

"Of the latter I cannot say. Of the document and its message, I can."

"Please do, revenant."

"Come close then," she said, in the lightest of voices.

He leaned her way, and her whispered words in his ears were madness and panacea.

Part IV
FIGURES

Across snows that fell lightly at times, heavily at others, Konrad made his way back to Sch^nbach and Ursula, who would drink deeply of such news as he bore. Only one in the world besides himself and the revenant knew the parchment's meaning and surely that individual was the boy Rein, who had brought the script to Carmen, then known as Laila, for translation. Even so, what could one do with such knowledge but cherish it? That and pass it along to one's loveless lover and hope it broke all barriers for good.

She was standing in the doorway with a rare smile on her face when he emerged out of the forest on his spherial. Time, in its way, paused as they remembered each other to the detail over the whiteness. She had a look about her which resembled his own, though he had never known her to express excitement, or any other emotion that exceeded certain boundaries. Konrad chose not to dwell on the strangeness however, preferring to embrace it. If she would but keep that smile until he reached the door...

Her hand in his was warmer than he had ever experienced, her lips...now on his cheek, his jaw, his mouth...beautiful as he'd ever imagined.

"Come," she kept saying. "I told you before you left there was something I wanted to share with you. You must look before it's gone forever. Eventually," she said, "things do that. Disappear forever. Don't you do that, Konrad."

"I won't," he promised.

And he entered his house again, skin against her skin.

She took him directly to her laboratory, opening the door as if the spaces behind had never been off-limits to him, as if...she finally trusted him. When he saw the thing he held his composure, diverting his eyes to her, trying not to conclude that he was the most convenient audience, that this so longed for moment with her was not about either of them, but some monster she had created out of the dust of former ages.

"I know you saw the train," she said to him. "I know you realize that Carmen's body was developed from a recovered DNA sample of a young girl on that train. What you are looking at now was derived from the strand of one who delivered the scrolls to the train's occupants."

Konrad stared at the writhing monstrosity before him, for a moment finding among its folds two eyes of green fire.

"Aen," he said, a word gone in its own utterance.

"I have never encountered such a cell structure," she said. "Twice I have built the creature and twice it has died. The last time I was able to revive it. What you see is that resurrected version. Is it not the most amazing thing you have ever witnessed?"

I have witnessed such things, Ursula. I have witnessed such terrible things.

He saw the disappointment, the disconnection in her eyes…for the experiment was the most personal thing about her, to be shared with him…

"I love you, Ursula. Kill it, and love me back."

A flash of something so red that it had no known source. Then, for the first time in eternity, she cried.

In her room her hands found his hair, his face, his eyes, yet other parts she would not touch. When he wondered why, she told him to wait. Always the waiting. But in this case he did not have to do so for long. A knock came at the door out of the night. When he told her to ignore it, she put her finger on his lips.

There at the stoop lay two piles of snow. She knelt before one, hands making magic over its contours as Konrad watched his very personage take shape beneath them. His own attempt at sculpture proved more awkward than hers, but sufficient for the task. Their molded figures moved into the depths of the house, igniting in the magnificent silence, shushing for a time the orchestrations of memory.

Though somewhere, in the beautiful midst of it, he thought he saw multiple sets of eyes looking down on him, multiple pairs of hands cradling his small body. Or were those hers, wandering the hidden spectrum of the flesh, delicate as the darkness spinning them in its ancient silk…

The Tiptoeing Monk

345 post auroram
(64th century, Gregorian calendar)
Huna Glacier, Southeast Alaska

Part I

1

Closing the book, Kai looked around him at the frozen walls of his home. Though the cave burned a brilliant and spectral blue as its material refracted the rays of the low sun, a stage it was not; nor all the world. But you mightn't have known such by the incessant chanting of the children outside:

> *Into no future and out of no past*
> *The tiptoeing monk, his shadow is cast*
> *Away through the ice, across a bleak sea*
> *The tiptoeing monk, he carries the key*

Incessant and unbearable, and yet the entire choir his: in their love of words as closely as in blood. All the world a stage indeed. For its ragged clans encased in ice? Language stopped making sense there.

> *The tiptoeing monk, he carries the key*
> > */what key?/*
> *The key to other than were*
> > */what key?/*
> *The key to other than were*

Kai looked at the volume in his hands and wondered if anything could have ever been netted out of its obscurity. He thought to bring the question to his wives, but knew that Taneidí would accuse him of philosophy, Karmiti of pastime, Naqi of hope. They'd point out that the clan had never even considered such nonsense until he had begun prowling around the library—a clan unto itself.

He hoped for the sake of their musical children out there—Adriel, Taima, Anoki, Dyami, Huna, Tala, Shakespeare, Little Edensaw—that not only the clan, but the whole tribe would eventually regard the library as part of its structure instead of just another relic unearthed out of the melting ice. The battle between inquiry and taboo seemed endless, as if all time indulged in selfish anticipation. Such was the life in Alaska, the flotsam of what had once been.

Kai placed the book in its empty slot in the fissure wall. Beside it was another collected works: *The Bible*. Strange book, that. Beside it again was a tome that bore only the title *The End of What Is* and did not apologize for the fact with an author's name. Only Shakespeare was so vain among the three volumes. Only Shakespeare made any sort of sense, in any practical terms, as distant as was his language. The fissure kept the books well in any case. They were texts out of time. So said the tiptoeing monk:

> *Into no scripture and out of no script*
> *The tiptoeing monk, his secret is kept*
> *The Bible, the Shakespeare, the End of What Is*
> *A vault of dead knowledge and all of it his*

Kai considered calling the children in and waxing inspirational upon them again, but what was more inspiring than song, otherwise lost and forbidden among the undigested bones of time? The song was the butterfly; the music, the vapors of vomit seeping out of the relics. Kai had pulled the three books out of the Library *because* of the surviving chant, had he not? Fascinating that they had been displayed there together, on their carved easels of wood and leather, as though exalted in a reeking/wreaking drama of memory.

Where had man been to be forced to dwell here?

What had he done?

Ah, but that advocate for oblivion, that symbol of the arcane, the tiptoeing monk knew. It was May again, according to the calendars of ancient days, and that saboteur of childhoods was silently but certainly afoot. If only there *were* such a keeper, and such a key. If only the days didn't blur in glacial blue, the jagged shards of ruin protruding at all angles from it. If only there were someplace to go. Like the children did.

Kindling the stove, Kai watched their movements outside the mouth of the cave and maybe the world was a stage after all. One of his own sons had been named Anoki, after the original meaning, 'actor'. The boy was every bit of that as he twirled his sister—a wisp of flesh in icy translucence—in his magic fingers, and as she in turn twirled Tala, and Tala, Huna, and Huna, Little Edensaw, and the chant like the call of the wilderness surrounding:

> *The tiptoeing monk, he carries the key*
> > */what key?/*
> *The key to other than were*
> > */what key?/*
> *The key to other than were*

Anoki, after the original meaning. Funny, the word *after* stood out every bit as bizarre as the word *actor* in the final dissolution of time. Little matter in the end, such thoughts, as the bands of the spectrum deepened in the walls. The fire crackled hideous faces up through the chimney and the smell of fish invited without words. As eight children gathered around the salmon, Kai spared a thought for a ninth, his eldest, out in the wild hunting.

Deep into spring and the weather still cold.

"Tell us, father!" cried the eight as Kai filled their plates. "Tell us about the tiptoeing monk's secret!"

Cold. The seductive May sun splintering among the agonizingly slowly diminishing sculpture of existence.

"The tiptoeing monk," began Kai. "He knows the way out of the desolation and to a new place…"

II

It was what it was, the season: the snow and the air and wind. Sleep knew the season better than wakefulness, and all things that transpired did so without the permission of the conscious mind. Kai was caught tearing at the mosaic of his flowing hair when out of the endless indigo, from the world and stage at large, emerged the voice of his firstborn son Dúrin:

"Father, I have found it! The key!"

It was a nightmare, yet it lived.

"The Monk's key, father!"

To all that was, and had never been, and would never be. The biting dog of the present in the strewn wreckage of the past.

"The *monk's* key?" Kai fashioned a look to complement his unimpressed baritone.

"Yes, yes, I know it's a symbol, father. But I am telling you I have found the actual *physical* symbol."

"Where?" asked Kai.

"The monastery of course. Where the Compound never thought to look."

He referred to the strata of survival in the region; a chronological and anthropological cross-section of natives, spiritual isolationists, survivalists anticipating the fall of principal America, and refugees created from that very eventuality... swollen and symbolic themselves. The monastery, built upon a landscape's potential near the end of the Gregorian nineteenth century, had entertained them all. People had lived and died for said landscape, ever-shifting though it was.

And yet here was Dúrin, with the end to wonderment. The key. The Monk's own key.

"Where the Compound never thought to look?" Kai echoed dubiously. "It was from among its members that we got the supplemental, handwritten afterword I found in *The End of What Is*. One would assume they explored their subject matter with as much thoroughness as enthusiasm."

"Hundreds staring in the face of the long winter descending? A legend that preceded their arrival? Monks in a wasteland? This does not even construct a fantasy, much less something they would actually go out and risk trying to confirm."

"Is the thing on your person?"

"It is at the monastery."

"There can be no actual key," said Kai. "It is a nursery rhyme. Yes, the

Compound believed it, but they were without hope at the end of the world."

"Put on your clothes and come with me, you stubborn man."

~

The monastery lay below the glacier, across what had once upon a time been a lake that had frozen in the winter and thawed in the spring, in keeping with the cycle of things. Exceedingly well preserved, the artifact nestled in a pocket in the mountainside, beyond the Compound and the library and upon the built-in totems and glyphs of the indigenous Huna Tlingits. The series of overlapping relics was a bruised onion of the past, the distinctions between layers hard to identify. It might have been the monks who built the library; it might have been the survivalists. The truth lay deep and unattainable among the rotting skins.

"A tiptoeing monk is a very specific idea," Kai passed ahead to his son as they left behind the last shelves of the library, delving into the more profound shadows of the monastery.

"It is that, father. As a child, I was terrified of him. Your fault of course, with your habit of ignoring taboo to widen our horizons."

Kai felt Dúrin's smile through the dark. A silent thank you where the gentler emotions seldom found expression.

"Son, what made you look for such an abstract thing in the first place?"

"I don't explore only for meat, father. You taught me better than that."

"So I did," Kai said.

"Watch ahead here. The path turns sharply to the right. We don't. You will find me on the other side of the hole before."

"But I see no hole."

"Exactly."

It needn't be explained, for Dúrin's hand was there to guide him into a darkness that even Kai's probing *knuckle-eye*, set in his glove, failed to penetrate. *A key in here?* he thought, shining his narrow beam into nothingness. It was good he had a grown son for such pursuits now.

"Do you see anything?" said Dúrin.

"I don't."

"Close your eyes, father."

Kai did, for he was the student here, sire or no.

"Now tilt your head back and look above you."

He did that too, and the darkness compensated for his suspicion. In the fabric evolved a moon, silver and cratered. In the moon developed something else, a skeleton of shadow, a fairy-told key against the shining two-dimensional disc. Kai stared at the coin, and the negative image could not be mistaken. He sighed where sighs were inappropriate.

"If that is your key, Dúrin, I am forced to admit I don't care. In these times existence has no patience even for itself."

"This is your response, father? Philosophy?"

In the darkness, movement, drawing Kai's gaze from symbol to suggestion. That of a hood, of eyes. Perhaps even a snout, at the cusp of the senses...

Father found son's eyes, youthful fear lurking there as Dúrin, too, had discovered possibility in the darkness. And yet, upon deeper inspection; nothing but the violation of the knuckle-eye in the gloom. Even the symbol had dissolved.

III

"It was the monk himself, that is sure," said Dúrin. "A hundred times I have visited the place and never encountered more than my own shadow, my own footfalls."

"My eldest is mad, then?"

"You saw the key, father. What about the key?"

"What *about* the key, son? What use is a silhouette to me or the tribe in general, except as more fodder for superstition? It is the symbol, I concur. But it has no purpose among us."

"It is more than the symbol, father. The light, the shape of light actually led me to a metal key imbedded in the rock beneath it. I came back the first time with the idea, then the next time with a hammer and pick. I imagined the key in a sort of light relief, and there, in the rock, it was. Would you like to see it?"

They were in the interim between monastery and library now, enticed out of the obscurity by knowledge known, as opposed to sought. "I have to see it," said Kai.

"Of course. I delayed because I felt it better to show you the how before the what."

"Shut up and show me the damn thing."

Dúrin produced a small metallic object, extending it on his palm to his father.

Kai studied it, frowning. "It bears nothing of the shape that led you to it. Indeed it is shapeless."

"Quite the contrary. It has a very distinctive profile if you hold it against a contrasting surface."

Kai placed the silvery object against the dark fabric of his sleeve, tracing its edges in the beam of his knuckle-eye without much success. The naked gaze proved the better tool, as Dúrin's expression suggested Kai might have realized in advance. The latter said:

"It is the image of the tiptoeing monk himself."

"Indeed."

There was a protracted silence that only the ice could comprehend.

Kai found his eldest across the wintry profound. "Then the Compound created this key to further the monk's mystique?"

"Or the monk, to further the Compound's ideal."

"Our mystical and mythical monk."

"Take everything else away, father. All that we know and have known. All that we strive to know. And there is still one remainder: the monk. Does it really matter what form he takes as long as he produces? I have never told you this, but I have found passages in *The End of What Is* that simply were not there on previous inspection."

A chill born not of the ice visited Kai, for he had discovered the same. "Have you tried the key, son?"

"I have not. But I know where it goes."

Kai waited.

"The corridor in your own house where you keep your books."

Kai stared. "Corridor? You mean the *fissure*?"

"When I was young, you tried to burn off the ice where the fissure narrows to a vertical wink—you were curious to know if the cleft extended further. You concluded, because of the thickness of the ice, it did not. The whole process, the idea of a mysterious tunnel winding through the glacier fascinated me as a kid. And still does. I have traced a similar tunnel from this library to the mirror image of that vertical wink. I know it is the same fissure because of the depression just to the right of the seam. A depression whose configuration fits this key exactly. That strange imperfection—on each side of the 'door'—is and remains the only interruption in the smoothness of the ice. This despite the mutable nature of the glacier."

Kai waited, Kai stared, Kai marveled. "Have you *tried* the key, son?"

"From both sides of the door, yes. It cannot be accomplished with only the one key."

"There is…another?"

"Yes. The monk, I believe, carries it on his own person."

IV

It was a simple plan, contrived by simpler people for greater purposes. After some argument, which included the brandishing of his elder status, Kai eventually relinquished the role of the unarmed to defend the home side of the theoretical portal. Even so, they fashioned a key out of soft metal to give the appearance of believing the thing could be done so crudely. Kai felt foolish carrying the imitation key to his small hour rendezvous with his son at a door with no name, but he'd felt more foolish contemplating not doing so.

> *The tiptoeing monk, he carries the key*
> > */what key?/*
> *The key to other than were*
> > */what key?/*
> *The key to other than were*

What did such words mean? To tribal law, the monk might as well have been the cunning and seductive Satan of the Bible, or a Lady Macbeth after her own calculated ends. Secret was secret, and therefore taboo. The world had been destroyed by secrets; the world survived on ignorance. It was a cycle that neither Shakespeare nor the authors of the Bible had ignored. *The End of What Is* was another matter entirely, condemned to the furthest frozen spheres of the earth by the tribal council. It did not even warrant comment save that comment effuse contempt and fear.

So Kai and his son Dúrin, at a terrible and strange hour in the course of mankind, faced each the other's image in a split pocket of ice while eight children slept in their beds, three wives and mothers in theirs, and the promise of nothing and everything residing in the two-sided mirror before them. Through a quirk in the properties of the ice, the father actually visually perceived the son insert the placebo into the depression, though he could see nothing else of Dúrin's form. Unbeknownst to him, on the other side of the mirror, Dúrin also watched him as he placed the authentic key into its mold.

A simple trap. Laid for what neither regarded as simple quarry.

And yet the monk came as called. Kai leapt backward as he encountered the muzzled face in the ice before him. Only a moment to seek understanding before the aspect retrograded, simultaneously rotating to become the profile of a tightly helmeted, crouching medieval figure, knees bent deep as it tiptoed in the soft, silent history of its unshod feet. In its near arm it held a short broadsword, in the other, an undersized shield. A collar of mesh, perhaps mail, embraced the monk's shoulders, rendering him the picture in *The End of What Is* to the detail. All that lacked was the footnote attributing the image to a wood carving in some long lost church on Shakespeare's continent, of which *The End of What Is* spoke much.

Europa survives, whispered the head in the ice as it turned his way again. *It seeks to restore the puzzle pieces of civilization.*

Kai found himself staring as one does upon one's altered reflection in a flawed looking glass. The face that now regarded him was not the same one that had startled him upon its first appearance, though that of the bear peering from within a monk's cowl was just as common to the pages of *The End of What Is* as the incarnation of the battle-ready monk. The stray tendrils of hair that escaped the medieval helmet caught against the monk's steady prosaic face in a wind that also rendered the strands glacial blue.

"We have the roots of civilization here," said Kai. From the other side of the portal, where he sensed Dúrin experienced the encounter in mirror image, he thought he heard his son groan.

The monk did not dally in expression: *You speak of were. I speak of other than were.*

"Are you the harbinger of hope then? Is it that simple?"

I am he who passes through all things. In some quarters I am called Fane; in others, Aen. Here, I am the Tiptoeing Monk.

The words of Dúrin, somehow filtering through the frozen door: "We *seek* other than were. We seek the guidance of the Tiptoeing Monk."

The bear's muzzle yawned into a maw, teeth shining in icy brilliance.

Recognizing that the world was about to change forever, Kai begged of the monk a goodbye to his children.

If you are here, at the door to which I carry the key, said the monk, *then the goodbyes have been said. In other than were it scarcely matters.*

"Are they not families there, too?" Kai challenged.

They are families and brothers and lovers and madmen, like here. But it is there, not here, that the ultimate key lies. I offer the glimpse into other than were. Such has always been my occupation, even before I was aware of it. Were is possibility, Other is beyond the conceptual, though it is a landscape, away through the ice and across a bleak sea, at the near extent of my shadow. Fear not. The Tlingit people, neither Raven tribe nor Eagle feared the bear. The salmon did not fear the bear. The monks did not fear the bear, even when it ran wild among them. The library did not fear the bear even when it sat at a table amongst the tongues of strayed knowledge and proclaimed itself a flower.

As he said the last he unfurled the prize in his paw/delicate hand, holding it aloft for that instant, then passing it through the ice to Dúrin, who placed it into its mold without bothering to remove the placebo.

A black rape upon the bands of the spectrum, and the seven winds told on tricks and tricksters.

Part II

1

It was a strange and contradictory landscape that presented itself out of the prism. In the foreground occurred the flutter of what Kai recognized as swans about their nesting; in the background, the pearly white edges of an old and lovely city half sunk into the sea. A diluted photograph strangely aglitter in moonlight, the scene was beyond the touch, the actual physical contact of the senses. It might have been a dream but for the words behind it:

Brugge: a coastal city of the former country of Belgium. A Venice of the North to rival both Amsterdam and St. Petersburg, it was once famous for its swans. As you see, they still survive, in their enhanced but still ever graceful, natural forms.

"Enhanced?" queried Dúrin, out of his sphere within spheres.

Enhanced genetically. The world neither died nor survived without effort.

"And here in Alaska?" posed Kai. "Are *we*, too, genetically…enhanced?"

There in Alaska. We travel now. And no, you hadn't the chance. The Raven and the Eagle tribes survived as they have always done. You benefited from that as displaced Americans.

"From that and a monastery, it seems." Kai's will was his aura.

I have a roof under which to sleep, as you have.

"Why?" asked Dúrin. "Why hadn't we the chance?"

Because America was swept up in the very flare that signaled its emergency, leaving ash. While the cataclysm that destroyed the world began and ended in Europa, it found its poetic instant on your continent, consuming all of America's science and technology, all its armory, all its body and soul in a biblical day. With the exception of Europa, a doomed piece of land known as Israel, and an island or two off the coast of infamy, the forces of the whole earth were against her. In her great appetite, she had used up most everything that lay within her reach. Eventually she used up herself.

All of which, Kai thought, was suggested in *The End of What Is*. The phrase "in the blink of an eye,"—Shakespearean? Biblical?—was used more than once in the references to America's fate. Dúrin knew as much. It was the deeper answer Kai knew his son sought. However posed, however uttered, *Why?* remained always an existential question. History had left room for no variety.

And so, this Brugge was not a city of swans, but a city half lost to the sea. Nor was it a sinking Atlantis, but an aviary, a picture upon time.

Dúrin pursued the next logical question: "That glittery substance on the air…?

Is the tinge aether, a toxic residue of the end of Europa. Brugge is not even spared that in the end.

Kai looked out beyond the bands of the spectrum to gemstone, midnight blue. The tiptoeing monk walked there, softly, on naked feet. His sword over his mouth momentarily as he gestured them on with his shield.

Not even spared that in the end.

The Monk had loved the place once. Such was clear. But not so much that he let it interfere with the next picture off his steely wand.

Why, son, why indeed…

~

Because.

Because I was there when the rain fell. All that falls now is us. We. Travelers.

This is the Gardasee, of the former country of Italy. They construct their homes out of the very rock upon which they walk, and toss the residue into the brilliant lake below. The town I know best, Tignale, survives as an artifact and as a rebirthed community because it was built high upon the steep banks of the lake. Look now on the water. Yes, sails. Sails in sunlight, so long forgotten. Sails. As if none of it had ever happened. As if the world might bloom again. As if our astral journey were as much about recreation as annihilation, whimsy as waste. But shhh, lest the orchestrator hear us. Lest we forget what our journey is truly about.

"Orchestrator?" echoed Dúrin. "What *is* the journey truly about?"

It is about the moon, that Roman token; the night, that clear green gem. It is about the snow, bleeding in. It is about the kiss of chromium and the caress of isolation. Find your way out of yourself and you will know.

"But you make no sense. *Who* is the orchestrator?"

Hasn't that always been the most delicate question, caught there between how and why? Who indeed. Who tunes the violin to its purest note? Who perfects the mathematics of architecture such that the earth balances upon the pin? Who carves and sculpts, of the wisps of souls, the most sublime countenances? Who hears the echoes of destruction long before the storm has landed and yet lets nature run it course with a wry smile on his face?

"God. You speak of God," said Kai. "I'd have imagined…"

Something less obvious? That, I cannot give you, though your answer is *inherently and fundamentally wrong. Neither God nor the Devil may make such a claim. Man. He* is *the orchestrator. You…are the orchestrator.*

Kai felt the anger surge, both in himself and in his son, questioner of journeys.

Their words became tangled as they both delivered upon their pilot at once.

"Survival? That is orchestration—"

"*Lets* nature run its course?"

These are the strokes of history. Man is history. Man is time. Man is an artist the likes of which even God mightn't have envisioned. But that betrays the point, which is that after all he has sown and reaped, Man still finds pleasure in his world. He still calls his children to dinner, remembering over the salmon the brother that is still out in the endless winter on the hunt.

All the world is his stage. All the world is yours. From this, the sumptuous belly of an Italy, an ancient Rome—

The scene flashed from is to is.

—to this:

Coiling, encrusted outgrowths over uneasily calm seas.

The volcanic coast of a France. This:

Dry rocky odes to missions that had since bled out on the desert floor.

Spain, where the sun ceased to shine only in myth. This:

The ice again. The snow. The...

Scandinavia, friend of your latitude. These:

Picks and spikes and determination.

Your people.

Settling for keys, mystic memories, visions of other than were.

Will you be deposited here where possibility folds upon itself, or go back to Alaska? My work as your monk is done. Why is a worthy question, but I am loath to be its answerer.

Because.

"My family?" said Kai. "Dúrin's mother? His siblings? They must be sacrificed for knowledge?"

The suggestion of the bear's muzzle again as it momentarily forsook the depths of the cowl. *In Aland they will guide. They are monks themselves, only of a different sort. Give them the key. They will know to what it strictly belongs.*

The key...look at its configuration again. Is it not of a long weary tree in driving wind and snow? Don't let it blind you. It welcomes you, she *welcomes you as survivors of a lost continent.*

II

She indeed. There was no description for her as she evolved of the snow, which itself had evolved of the tiptoeing monk's parting words. Her ghostly visage, at first glance, seemed as much a part of the veil of snow as of the personage bleeding through it. Her profile might have matched that of the key and it might not. Such obscurities seemed superfluous now. Snow fell in a palpable ballet around Kai and Dúrin, and the ground beneath their boots was textured and real. She was the specter, not they.

"Welcome," she offered out of the swirl. "Welcome to Aland. We have not known Americans since the end of civilization."

She wore a pale frock, and her eyes smiled from beneath her hood. When Dúrin held forth the key, she was impressed. "Ah yes. Surrealium slag. They sell it in Trier as if it means something, touting it to the pilgrims as 'concentrated tinge aether.' The material's actual nature remains unknown, though it is certainly to do with the end of the First Age and man's descent into ignorance. See how it captures the season in its simultaneous amorphousness and rigidity. What did Aen tell you about it? That it was the amber of the moon?"

Kai spoke half ironically: "He said something about Roman tokens and green gems. He last described the key as 'a long weary tree in driving wind and snow.'"

"Our tiptoeing Aen never ceases to be the poet. But come," said her briefly materializing features, "we are *your* kind."

Aen was not?

Kai found Dúrin as enchanted by the inherent elegance of the snow as he was. The dancing flakes seemed to form their own portraits, she among them.

"What is your name?" father and son said.

"Mavra. I have been here since before either of you were born."

III

She led them across a landscape as sleekly carved as their own Huna Glacier, but more sophisticated. Trees grew out of the very ice, orchards and fruits of the bands of the rainbow, and young people on the firn plucking them from the branch. The sky reflected the prismatic harvest in the metallic lining of its umbrella. The fruits were often too large for the tender hands of their gleaners, magnifying in the mirror of forgotten blue.

A door lay open as they arrived. A door upon a cave in a hill. A mouth.

Gesturing into the shining blue darkness, she said, "Here, we call it the North and East. Does that ring in some memory cell?" She was a gracious and patient hostess as she stood there, enshrouded.

"We wish only to understand the secrets of the key," said Dúrin, bringing all dimensions back into focus.

Mavra smiled, shaking her head. "The Tiptoeing Monk and his secrets. The key is obviously malleable. How to keep up with such landscapes, such possibilities? And yet, we do so here. Let me hold the key in my hand as we enter. It is something. Anything that bears the monk's scent is something. Did he tell you goodbye or did he tell you farewell? He comes and he goes, mostly goes. We welcome him, but then we also welcome the amber of the moon. You are that, are you not? Your own miracle in time?

"That is what we are about here in Aland. Our island's survival, itself, is a wonder of nature. Four thousand years have passed since the end of the First Age, and existence still centers here, in this far detached place in the mysterious North and East. Elsewhere, where the Tiptoeing Monk is known as Fane, they call this point in space and time that we are about to enter the Cavern Axendice. Those within regard it as a hub and crossroads of man's three paths of survival: Here, There, and Other Than Were. Or if you prefer: Fern, Firmament, and Friend. Fern representing man's bid here on Earth; Firmament, his escape to the stars; Friend…well, that is another question, isn't it? Look…is this the key after all…?"

It hung there on air, an image out of the fantasy of the father and the nightmare of the son, and vice versa, then fell bleeding a leaden chromium into the procession of snow, washed away by excess memory as much as tide. And the gaping mouth before.

"Why are *we* here?" said Dúrin.

"It is occasionally true that our sires must be sought from abroad. The propagation cycle depends on it. Within, you will better understand what form this cycle takes. I will allow you in advance that it would steal a part of you from your families forever. Such is the price of Aland."

She turned then, solidifying as she had not previously done and stepping into the luminous darkness of the cave.

As they followed her footsteps, Kai leaned down, picking up the smear of the key. For a moment, as he looked at it against the nothingness, he knew the glimmer of understanding. Then they entered the cave and nothing would ever be the same again.

Part III

1

A corridor led past blind passages in the rock. Tubes powered by an unknown source lit the way. Sculpture resided in niches in the wall, strange faces, strange figures just beyond the reach of the memory. An unnatural hum thrilled in the walls. The robe of their guide luminesced, opalesced, like a seashell in the flare of the fleeting sun. The floor seemed insubstantial beneath their feet as they progressed like vapor through another mouth in the rock and into a cavern.

In the midst of the vast natural hall, suspended aloft without any visible support, were six objects. Three were inanimate; the other three…it was not certain.

"What are they?" said Dúrin. His amazed whisper benefited threefold from the acoustics of the hall.

"They are," said Mavra simply, though with her own unsuppressed wonder.

The three inanimate objects were globes, of varied size and description. The largest, about five meters in diameter, clearly represented Earth—the encrusted, contrast-harsh Earth of now as opposed to the more colorful planet depicted by the archaic globes in the Huna Library. The second and third spheres, whilst failing to rival the mass of the first, spoke to faraway and exotic horizons wrought of their own distinctive outlines and textures and depths of blue.

Surrounding the globes, in a similarly independent fashion, hung three life-sized human forms. One was considerably taller than the others, though favorably proportioned; another wore what both Kai and Dúrin knew instinctively to be a period costume, though they could not have named the age represented; the third was the least humanoid, fully half of its body appearing to be fashioned— perhaps *sculpted* better fit—of snow.

"He is beautiful, is he not?" expressed Mavra. There was no question as to which figure she referred. Aland's coordinates were, after all, in the North and East.

"Then come," said she. As if a choice had been presented and decided upon.

One of multiple apertures in the far wall welcomed them into another, deeper corridor. The sculptures along the walls began to grow more grotesque, often of a wintry, perhaps even apocalyptic theme (though who knew the true meaning of such words). Faces howled out of blizzards; skin curled in horror, teeth flashed like knives through rope; eyes wept snowdrops, as gravity liked. Hieroglyphics appeared between the figures, knowledge of other hands, other perceptions, an alphabet serving journeys accomplished and journeys yet to be. Lilts bearing the grace of the sea; sweeps, the power of the incoming tide. It occurred to Kai and Dúrin simultaneously that they might be in a tidal cave. A dampness clutched all. The restless air tasted of brine. Mavra, for all her wonder speak, moved as with death on her person.

"Do you believe in the winter?" said she. "Or is it a word invented to describe what has happened to civilization?"

The walls sweated, the floor floated. "Where we come from," Dúrin said, "there is a preserved library, a relic of the First Age. I have read a measurable portion of its contents—perhaps unbeknownst to my father. Yes, the winter is real. And 'the end of civilization' hardly needs any other description. 'Blink' is the only term that has ever made sense to me when it comes to what occurred. 'In the blink of an eye'. That is real to me."

"In a blink you might be washed away in a blizzard," said Mavra. "In a blink you might fail or transcend those who love you. I despise the word."

Still, when they had blinked, they were out on an open rocky harbor. Surrounding the area were high banks of fresh snow, shovels protruding from the mounds here and there. Mavra extended a hand over the gray sea, pointing out that this was the path they were concerned with today. "The boatman will come….if you will but look…"

They did. And in the blink of an eye they were lost in history.

ll

At that nameless hour the city bell rang seven distinct times, signaling the opening of the seaward gates. When the last note had faded, Mavra's mother Emma wiped a poorly concealed tear from her eye, then took her daughter's hand, leading Mavra out into the wintry night. Bunched together in their cloaks against the driving snow, mother and daughter passed like shadows beneath clanging chimes, rattling shingles, rocking street lamps. The wind dragged at their feet on the paving stones, inspiring miniature whirlwinds of white dust as if to further obscure the night's doings.

As they neared the gates, the faces of other daughters, other mothers, appeared out of the blow—frightened, scrawled with uncertainty, facets of the mask of destiny. Six-year-old Mavra clung to Emma all the more tightly, having known for days that something was amiss but now sensing the essence of what was to come, secrets hinted at only in whispers. She had dreamed of the *Equiception*, that mysterious science they did not teach in base school, had seen the harbored vessel delivering cargo from some distant place. Observing the other daughters clutching their mothers, she suspected she wasn't the only one.

As the gates slowly lifted and the man with the seaman's coat stood there, it seemed the weather receded from him, opening up to a night dominated by a huge ghostly moon, its silvery ribbons swinging across the sea. He walked amidst the huddled pairs, measuring the daughters with his gray eyes. For a second Mavra felt his gaze on her, cool like the moonlit breath of the sea collecting over the dock behind him. She felt the shudder that followed the almost imperceptible whimper from Emma's lips. Then his gaze had moved on, searching the other forlorn silhouettes in the gateway.

Mavra and her mother held each other as desperately as Mavra had ever remembered. There was no hiding the tears any longer, not from each other, not from the boatman, whose extended finger now accompanied his stare as he began to select from among the scattered pairs of mothers and daughters. Mavra watched in dismay as his very gesture seemed to cause grief and desolation, mothers engulfing their daughters in their cloaks, quavering over them as over the dead. This time she and the boatman locked eyes, a dark foreknowledge preceding the motion of his hand as he casually marked her. Somewhere behind the ice-keen moment of contact, Mavra heard Emma wail into the night, joining the other mothers of the chosen. Those who were ignored shuffled away, the women murmuring prayers as they pushed their children before them.

In the end eleven girls remained, the protective arms around them at last relaxing. Mavra joined the others in tearfully kissing their mothers for what they instinctively knew to be the last time before stepping beneath the teeth of the raised gates. By the time the dour procession reached the dock, there were only ten girls.

For Mavra had submerged herself in shadow.

The boatman beckoned them aboard, counting as he did. As each girl climbed on deck, one of the crewmen lifted a bloated sack onto his back. This went on, in the fashion of one sack for each passenger, until all ten girls were on the boat. When the last one had stepped off the ramp, the man in his dingy coat searched the area with his gray eyes. Mavra felt a terrible, consuming dread as they passed over her once, twice, then returned to fix her in their snare.

His finger seemed drawn on one of the ribbons of moonlight as it found her. Trembling, she emerged from her spot, answering the call of her beckoner step by dread step. When she reached him, he invited her on board in silence. She wouldn't look at his eyes as she stepped across the ramp. No sooner had she planted her feet on the deck than the boat began to rock with the weight of bodies climbing out of the vessel. She turned to watch the men with the burlap sacks file towards the gates, which still had not closed over the shadowy figures that stood there hugging themselves and clutching their mouths as if to stifle cries.

One of those figures was Emma.

Muttering that cherished name, Mavra ducked behind the last sack bearer, hiding in his hulking shadow until the appropriate moment and then leaping from the boat and fleeing across the beach. Through the whirling snow she ran, past the dock and ancient quay, beneath the crystalline cliffs that replaced the city wall along Imberlock's eastern projecting spur, into view of the blue glacier that formed the seaward rim of the sweeping icefield of the north where none were welcomed and all soundly put to sleep.

As she dared invade the freezing wilderness which *had* been a part of her base school learning, the ice-white northern hands reached down delicately to collect her into their regions. The ghost wolves, smelling her fear, snarled and gathered but seemed to know not to begrudge her whatever she had come for.

Which might have been nothing had she turned back upon the silvery mist of her passage before sighting the object jutting out of the ever-shifting contour of high ground hemming in the glacier on the west, a gleam where there had previously been none, some revived relic of the lost ages…

~

Faces of various types occupied the train car: the anxious, the disturbed, the overwrought, the hopeless; yet all sharing the common thread of disquiet. A boy with strange blue hair passed out scrolls to the car's passengers. *Do not fear*, the boy told them. *There will be a new beginning. These conflicts of your world will very soon be a thing of the past. Absorb these written words I offer you. Your eyes will not recognize them, nor your conscious mind be able to interpret their message, but the older part of you, the part that lived before your Terran existence, will understand.*

The boy raised fiery green eyes to look at Kai and Dúrin. For a moment there was the suggestion of something more, something almost bestial…then the boy placed a finger on his lips, shushing the orchestrations of memory.

III

As the boat approached from the south, Mavra stood between her guests, caressing them with the moonlit quality of her words. "They will remember you as easily as they will forget you. Your family will cry, and those tears will be bottled for memory's sake. You will not be memorialized, you will not be canonized, you will not be idealized. In the end we are only what we are: particles in the bloodstream of the earth."

"I do not believe that," said Dúrin.

"Nor I," said Kai.

"Oh? You've a better purpose? Tell me, each of you, which flake among the blizzard are you?"

Kai and Dúrin fell silent, watching the vessel complete its approach, gently pulling alongside the moorings. A guttural roar from some unknown location, some sinister origin, caused the two crewmen to look up briefly from the business of securing the ropes to scan what would have been a ghost harbor but for the three personages scrawled out of the whimsical indecisions of moon and snow.

The crewmen disappeared momentarily, then reemerged leading two small hooded figures who peered over what might have been muzzles as they tiptoed across the planking, fiery green eyes laughing at the nature of creation, youthful bodies exuding an aura of hymns and dirges coalescing in ripe irony against the melting pockets of tomorrow.

And last, the captain, an ancient figure on the moonlit dock, gaunt from the endless seasons. His eyes, as they fell upon Kai and Dúrin, contained the cool breath of the sea; each of his weathered hands, an open burlap sack gathering shadows.

Disapparency

Four days ago Sarah, who works in the cubicle adjacent to mine, became one of them. On Wednesday she was looking at her telescreen, asking of its shades, "What are your thoughts, generally, concerning the War on Terror and, more specifically, the government's handling of it?" On Thursday the afterimages of the screen's shades, which might as well have been the shades themselves, were looking at her empty seat. There was just that sort of passivity to it all. Our supervisor's reaction when I inquired on Friday as to her whereabouts: "If you were doing your job, you wouldn't even miss her."

The trouble was, I did miss her. I missed the way she adjusted her mouthpiece before speaking into it. I missed the way she puckered her lips to conceal her sympathy when the phantom on the screen stammered its answer. I missed the simultaneously shy and sly smile she cast me every time I uttered something that broke the drone of fingers on keys, the sibilant monotone of soliciting voices, the repetition of the whole dreadful process.

Which is why I decided to do the unthinkable and go looking for the exact point in time when she shifted from our ranks to theirs—from the apparent to the unapparent, as I once heard it described. Once upon a time a disappearance— there, I've said the word—fell firmly into the category of the *more than apparent.* Now they were hardly missed. Or *if* missed, then secretly so.

At 6:30 on Friday afternoon I stepped over to her terminal, ejected the memory card (which I wasn't surprised to find still there, as it served merely as a backup) and replaced it with a bad one. What I was about to do simply wasn't done. But I was finished, finally, with maintaining my own passive countenance.

II

There is a cast about the faces of those who will be absorbed into the legion of the disappeared. It is like a foreboding, but not so—the mantle of fear, though that isn't right either. Guilt? That is closer to it. But not guilt for actions done, rather for those *not* done. For remaining passive, for looking the other way as their fellow citizens dematerialize almost before their very eyes. I had recognized the shadow on Sarah's face, but I'd preferred to think it a casualty of her occupation, a reflection from the telescreen and those aspects superimposed upon one another and melding into the white noise between apparent and unapparent.

But it is misleading to *attribute* the cast they wear. There is almost something inherent about it, as though its imprint existed before birth. Consider the very first face that appeared on my laptop after I'd settled into the comfort and privacy of my apartment and inserted Sarah's card. I could see that it was haunted even before Sarah finished introducing herself as an employee of the Attainable Future Group, an independent research company. As practiced as Sarah was at that word *independent*, I still detected a hesitation in her voice. The woman she spoke to, on the other hand, answered the question of questions with admirable poise, exhibiting not even the faintest trace of unease. Yet the cast was there, imbedded in her features, one with her. And maybe that is where my theory fails. Maybe the cast is a separate thing altogether, delivered by a certain light and attaching itself to the face like a parasite. While the cast comes in every shade from the karmic to the concessionary, the only certainty seems to be the ignorance of the victim. Though who hasn't looked in the mirror and wondered?

The second marked face among the succession of faces was not so cool. A scholarly looking man in his middish thirties, he stumbled over his answer to the point of embarrassment. Had I not immediately perceived what was, in his case, an aura of outright doom, I'd have deemed him a scared, piteous fool. Words like "necessary" and "sacrifice" spilled from his mouth even as he sought to retract them. In the end he broke down beneath the weight of his own words, babbling in anger-fright about sprawling prisons in the desert where innocent people were taken, never to be heard from again.

"I'm joining the Dems right now! Today! Should have done so long ago!" An assertion that might as well have been directed at the beam over which I envisioned him throwing a noosed rope before stepping off a chair. It was far too late in the game now to take up with the Demonstratives, whose survival philosophy amounts to being twice as vocal, twice as visible as the Evangelical Army, which parades in front of the Capitol at least twice a month, waving its banners gloriously.

The third face to emerge out of Sarah's calls from that last day of her *apparency* had a cast of an entirely different sort. It was neither an immediate nor a certain read, but ultimately it was a more chilling one. The lady was sternly attractive and pale, with closely cropped raven hair and a mouth that easily turned the question of questions around on the solicitor: "Are you sure you know to whom your question is directed? What do *you* think about the War on Terror? What do *you* think about the government's handling of it?" I imagined Sarah suddenly reflecting the wan visage in front of her, lips losing all their blood as her heart lapsed in its duty. I envisioned her thawing like one of her cold calls, the piercing sirens of a meltdown toxin filling the hissing white space.

"Ma'am, I-I am not in a position—"

"It doesn't have to be like this, you know."

"Excuse me?"

"There is a saying: 'Light is the touch of the turbaned man.' Do you remember light, Sarah? You are not alone. Meet me at seven this evening on the corner of 11ᵗʰ and Holland in front of the cell phone shop. Please come alone."

Reality threatened to come unwound as the sirens reached maximum pitch. I could not have heard Sarah's response even if she had given one. But I could see her face, in the screen, bloodless and austere, that of a nun too many years in the monastic crypt tending to dust.

"Until then," said the lady, out of the din. She might have been speaking to me.

III

I arrived at exactly seven, glancing around expectantly before entering the still open phone shop. The man behind the counter was Asian, in his fifties, likely the proprietor. I considered offering him a twenty, to be paid upon delivery of the information I sought, and then did. When I described the women to him, a strange look came over his face.

"You know them?" I interrupted myself.

"How can I forget two such pale creatures? Like angels fallen to Earth. There one minute then gone. Taken back up to heaven."

The chill didn't stop at the end of my spine.

"How do you mean?" I said.

"How do I mean? I mean I turn my head for only a moment and when I look again, they have disappeared. I go outside to look—it is not often one encounters angels, yes?—but they are nowhere. They have simply vanished."

This time the chill was dull, an after-tremor at best as it followed the necessary path. While I believed in *disapparency*, I did not believe Sarah had caught a heavenbound chariot right there in front of the gentleman's business. Even so, as I emerged from the store I pictured the two of them standing beneath the streetlamp, Sarah a hologram, already glimmering out. As the traffic bled through, I wondered where they had gone, the girl that worked in the cubicle adjacent to mine and the stranger who had offered…light? I looked around, appraising where one could go so quickly. Across the street was not possible, not in a 'moment' as the shopkeeper had described. Wherever they had gone, it had to be on this side of the street, and the only place within vanishing distance was the little tea shop next door. Its dark windows seemed to support its potential for intrigue even as they suggested the caller was at the wrong place, particularly at this hour. I didn't doubt the shop was open, however. Did those sprawling prisons in the desert shut their doors to visitors?

I went in without preparation. In this game surely there was none sufficient. As the aromas of the shop greeted me, so did a voice, husky but warm, a perfect extension of its owner. She was round with shortish straw hair, splotchy pink cheeks and a slight hairlip. Her smile was genuine as she paused from the book she was reading to offer me good evening. After I reciprocated she asked, "How may we help you today, sir?"

Are you privy to the exact point in time when Sarah Verdon disappeared from the ranks of the apparent?

I glanced beyond her at a curtained doorway leading into the deeper sanctum. A bouquet of orange and mint and lemon hung on the air. The title of the book she read suddenly registered. *The Infidel: A Look at the Dynamics of Eastern Extremist Hatred.* There was music playing, lightly, but seemingly in only one ear. From the speakers in the opposite wall issued what I could just make out as a crowd-rousing speech from an Evangelical Army demonstration. The two sounds blended well, in spite of having to share the same space. It struck me, quite in tune with the kaleidoscopic influx of impressions, that the music in my left ear was a chorus of *Onward Christian Soldiers.*

These thoughts were ephemera. A moment—time enough to disappear— might have passed since the woman's greeting. No more than that. I looked at her patient face and forgot what caution lingered. "Sarah Verdon," I said. "You took her from me."

Smile remaining fixed, she paused to allow her eyes to search mine before responding, "You believe her destiny to be coincident with yours?"

A difficult question with a strangely easy answer: "I do, actually."

"And yet," came a voice from behind the curtain, "she was the only one selected."

"*Selected?*" I said as the face from Sarah's call log emerged.

"Of course," she said, and extended a hand across the register, across the room and into my unready grasp. As I acknowledged her flesh in mine, I felt the silent rustle of the curtain reconfiguring behind me and we were in a dimly lit hall that seemed to tunnel into oblivion.

"Is this the way then?" I said. "From life? From liberty? From the pursuit of happiness?"

"From illusions?" she intoned, in my own inflection.

"From hope?" I countered.

"This is not the future."

"What is it then?" I said.

"It is the way to the future."

"So said Adolf Hitler."

Her chuckle was lost along the corridor.

IV

Where are you taking me?

I am taking you to the beginning, that exact instant in time.

Will I be able to see her?

Of course.

Will I be able to touch her?

She has already been touched.

My eyes opened from the retained essence of sleep, and the corridor extended before me, wall lamps diminishing into infinity.

"Do not worry. She is still there. Very small. Very impressionable. But is that what I mean, after all? Are we so corrupt? Such cavorters? Do you horde *your* feelings concerning the War on Terror? The government's handling of it? Are we talking about babies or disintegrating bones? Are they one and the same? Have you blindfolded yourself as instructed?"

"I have," I said, remembering only lamplight-tinged blackness as long as I'd been in her company.

"Don't fear what you see. Embrace it. But also go lightly. They are so young."

"So young," I echoed.

"You may remove your blindness at any time without repercussion."

"My blindfold?"

"Are you wearing one?"

"I don't know what you mean."

"Yes, remove it now. Precisely now. This point in time."

V

I opened my eyes to find myself in a neonatal ward. Newborns surrounded me, accusing with their squinted eyes, inquisitive in the language beneath the vocal spasms. I had nothing to offer, and yet they watched me as I began to move among them, watched me as though I had some key to the miserable and maddening journey they were about to embark upon. Their demands on my ears increased progressively, my ability to fulfill their wishes decreased equally progressively. Until…I saw *her*. Her puckering infant lips, as if she already had a distaste for life.

Where was my guide as I went directly to the baby Sarah and placed my finger on her brow? The light seemed to surface in her soft skin, as of its own device. She gooed and she gurgled and maybe she did neither as I retreated along the path between the infants, inadvertently finding the mirror behind them and the image of a turbaned man in my face.

I opened my mouth to deny…I don't know what, my own existence? But then they were there with cuffs and a cell number and the smell of the desert about their grim suits.

The Third Stanza

I often wonder why they came to me with their madness. Sure, I'm considered an expert in certain areas by those who read my books, and yes, I've been hired on as a consultant from time to time. But never on a project like this, of this scale and for such lofty reasons—maybe the loftiest of all. But this is as much a comment on my selling out to the EA, which I have despised since I was old enough to know how to despise, as it is a philosophical story. Let me take you back a bit, to a time when the notion of the literal Second Coming of Jesus Christ, even to the Evangelical Army, was a static one…

The Innermost Secrets of the Evangelical Army was my second book and the one that launched my career. I'll not pretend the book's success was due to anything other than the controversy surrounding it, of which there was plenty. Needless to say, the Evangelical Army, itself, was none too pleased with my look at what had almost become a state religion. I didn't care. I retained, I suppose, a fair amount of the revolutionary spirit of yore, that and an attitude of recklessness no doubt inherited from my American ancestors. Truth known, I *craved* causing some magnified version of the ripples I stirred among friends and acquaintances when I voiced my political opinions in their presence. I dared the authorities to come out and address the issues everyone was thinking about but no one spoke to.

In one sense I succeeded beyond my wildest imaginings. The book was a bestseller; the hard right practically took up arms in response, and the country's 'situation,' for lack of a better word, was laid bare on the cutting block. In another sense, and a very real one, my calling them out unified them, made them know that there were still some free thinkers and open minds among the populace—those, for example, who opposed the absoluteness of the War on Terror. The EA's unity, in turn, assured not only the validity of the War on Terror, but also its status as a practically omnipotent entity unto itself.

Ergo, success turned into a dichotomy that over the course of time nearly tore me apart. Guilt became as much a part of the mix as the sense of accomplishment, the personal validation, etc. From my point of view, the world changed, again, because of me. Whether that is true or not, I don't know. Maybe it's hubris. Maybe it's the madness, the infectious madness. When they came to me I laughed. Within three days I was in the employ of those I despised. Now I despised myself.

And why did I sell out? Because I wanted to see the Second Coming of Jesus Christ as much as everyone else.

II

Well, not everyone else. The Mormons, for example, cried foul because the Savior did not land in Jackson County, Missouri, as prophesied. The Seventh Day Adventists did not appreciate the fact that He announced His presence on a Sunday instead of a Saturday. And the Jehovah's Witnesses of course had already seen Christ's Second Coming, back in the early twentieth century. But by and large the Christians were tuned in and salivating copiously.

The Catholics were the key to it all. As shallow and over simplistic as it seems to voice out loud, they still held power in a global sense. They had numbers in Europe; they had mystique; they had a figurehead recognized the world throughout. When eventually I suggested as much to the man who appeared out of the blue at my Stuttgart, Germany residence one afternoon, introducing himself as Byrd with a 'y', representative of the Evangelical Army, his skepticism was plain. But that was later, after they had me in their snare. The initial conversation might have been extracted right out of a bad movie script. After the introductions and niceties, it went something like this:

"So what can the author of *The Innermost Secrets of the Evangelical Army* do for the Evangelical Army, Mr. Byrd with a 'y'?"

"We are working on a project that we feel you might be of some help with."

"Indeed? And what sort of project might that be?"

He became uncomfortable in his suit of tailored wool and self-assuredness, his ostentatious bald head gleaming in the foyer light as it adjusted to his response. In spite of his squirming, the words came this simply:

"We intend to trigger Armageddon."

I wouldn't let myself give him the satisfaction of a smile, though humoring him was a rare pleasure. "And just how do you intend to do that, Mr. Byrd?"

"By arranging the Second Coming of Jesus Christ."

I wouldn't have liked him even if he wasn't an agent of the EA. He was bloated and smug, characteristics undoubtedly earned through his faith. I let myself not only smile now, I laughed at him. "And this you will do how? Hymns and prayer?"

"Planning and ingenuity. That's where you come in, Mr. Moller. We have the actor, we have the production team, now we need the writer."

As I said, a bad movie script.

"I am qualified for this how?"

"You are an expert on the psychology of people. The Second Coming is the business of people."

"I see. And what, pray, would I get out of this?"

"A small fortune. The satisfaction of knowing you that you have manipulated the masses."

"I have both already."

"Both already," he laughed, suddenly getting back his game in all its arrogant glory. "Touché, sir. Touché."

I bowed slightly, a gesture for the idiots. The conversation had run its course. "It's a fine plan, Byrd, truly. But unfortunately it is one I must decline to be a part of."

"Is the world, as it is, so much to your liking?"

"Are you referring to the world in which the Evangelical Army exists?"

As he regarded me I thought the word 'touché' would leave his lips again. It was to his general well being—dubious as that was—that it did not. Instead, he pulled a card from his pocket. "Call me after you have thought it over."

"Good day, Mr. Byrd," I said, ignoring the extended bedroom pass to my enemies.

~

The next conversation, which took place the following morning on my porch, took a more sinister tone.

"I'd hoped you might call," he said, glancing at the garden table where he had dropped his card upon making yesterday's inglorious exit. There it still lay, undisturbed, next to my morning coffee.

"I'd hoped *you* might understand plain English."

"Alas, I am Italian, sir."

"Really? With a name like Byrd and a kinship with radical Christian rightists, I'd have thought you Middle Eastern."

He chuckled. "I enjoy humor, Mr. Moller. Particularly of the odd variety. But I fear the two gentleman sitting in my car are not so receptive."

Having already noted his passengers, I fixed wholly upon my guest. "And I, Mr. Byrd—I assume you changed your name from Marado or something equally as obvious…?—I am not receptive to threats. Or are you simply too dense to realize that if your illustrious outfit had seen fit, I would have disappeared long ago? Was the muscle the marionette's idea or his masters'?"

"My father's father was American. A fine man, some have said, in spite of the fact. Mine are determined masters, Mr. Moller."

"And who did you say you represent again?"

"You are astute, sir. We will have a nice marriage, I think."

"Yes, like the Evangelical Army and the Vatican. Tell me, how was that pulled off exactly?"

"Rest assured, I am on the side of Christianity in general. That is why I believe our Lord and Savior should appear at some unlikely location like Guam or Jamaica or Morocco. What say you on the subject? For the sake of argument."

Though I knew that every Guam and Jamaica that issued from his mouth was carefully chosen, I think it was then, at that moment, that I began to feel the pull of my own strings. "For the sake of argument? I would have his ship land right here in Germany. The Western subconscious would appreciate the symbolism of the Prince of Peace making his return appearance in the land of the greatest atrocities known to history."

"Yes. Yes, I see the logic. But the pope is German. Mightn't a showing in Germany give the impression that God favors the Catholic Church?"

I let the tick-tock man out as I regarded him with a blinkless, exaggeratedly tolerant gaze. He felt small in the silence, I could tell, but his gleaning that I did not suffer fools brought him no closer to the epiphany. I said, "You're not a friend of circumspect observation, are you, Byrd?"

"I have my moments," he said, shifting his eyes suggestively back to the Audi blocking my drive. The men inside the black sedan bristled as if in response.

"There are moments and there are moments, Byrd. Your masters are fools to try what they would now. This is not the twentieth century. The Second Coming of Jesus Christ? Better you try Walt Disney or Elvis Presley."

"They were unavailable, Mr. Moller. Clearly you need more time to think about your last wish. You still have my card—"

A loud noise interrupted him. I glanced to my right and saw a forklift reversing out of my neighbors' drive. It occurred to me only then that a lot of activity had begun over there as I visited with my friend from Italy. Lifting and moving and stacking, music of an addition to the house or some such.

I returned my attention to my guest, but he was already heading back to his goons with the apology. The card lay gleaming beside my cooling coffee.

~

In the end it was the Christ, Himself, who convinced me.

He was by no means Biblical as he and a virtual entourage stepped past me without invite into the interiors of my apartment that next morning, Mr. Byrd announcing him as "Jack Dabb, a long time coming." That this remark had any significance other than being a weak attempt at Christian irony on the part of my personal EA agent, I couldn't have known at the time. I let them sit in my living room, groupies and all, despite the uber-magnified smell of corruption. The strings, as noted, were already being plucked.

Before even the pleasantries were fully exchanged, one of the group was pulling from his trench coat an item that very closely resembled a tiny dog, though I was willing to attribute the yipping to my own neural alarm. As the disciple cupped it gingerly over my coffee table, Jack Dabb asked if I would bring a bowl of water. *Will he turn it to wine?* I wondered as I ambled off to do his divine bidding.

In the kitchen I heard the work from next door again, strange and isolated and noisy, nails driven into a coffin. I watched the tap water fill the bowl with a sense of things gone astray, moods not completely realized, time lost to its own insistency. Today the racket was more deliberate, angry, incessant. *My will be done.* The words of a poem from high school came to me, a juvenile affair with a sufficient meter, a predictable cadence, a less than subtle message.

> *I've haunted the brink of the murkiest well*
> *Where blow the worst storms, where work the worst spells*

I touched sweat on my forehead, drank from the bowl of water, filled it again. Something besides men and their schemes had entered my house today. The stench of it went beyond corruption, beyond deceit and treachery to the primaeval. The déjà vu it inspired went beyond the disconcerting to the terrible. I stood paralyzed in its grip, feeling simultaneously dejected and exalted, as if the secrets of the universe were only a retrieved breath away.

Byrd's voice penetrated the paralysis but not the stench, which oozed before me as I willed my muscles to obey his alien call: "Will you be joining us anytime soon, Mr. Moller? The demonstration is for your benefit, not ours."

The word *demonstration* rose out of the ancient mud and its miasma like a single tongue of fire, dancing before me toxically, intoxicatingly, beacon to some savage first enlightenment. As I entered the room they were all looking at me, not least the Christ, who now held the dog in His Own hands, in a secret, terribly familiar way. The yipping had been replaced by a strained whining, the extent of the animal's ability in such a primordial clutch. I wanted to cry out to the Old Testament God Who had invaded the New Testament Son, to beseech Him to spare the least of His children, but the thing was already recorded in the annals of the wretched Earth. Foam spilling over disillusioned fangs, nostrils flaring horse-like, eyes bulging as they captured the swamp flame in all its singular fury, fur retreating outward from the creature's clawing, frenzied body.

The sound of the lifeless animal dropping to the table accentuated a silence that still abides in me. My eyes found Byrd, standing slightly apart from the others, and as his own gaze returned…nothing, I realized that I had grossly misjudged him. Heaven did not suffer fools either as a lone but magnificent word issued from his lips:

"Behold."

I turned to the Christ looming over his deed. He looked at me, and as a nameless smile appeared on his lips, so did a knife in his hand. I'd a second to imagine the disemboweling of the poor beast before he turned the blade on his own flesh, opening his forearm. *This is my blood*, I heard in my own veins as I watched the fluid fall on the dog where it lay in its cruel little heap. The silence quaked, but for all its power it was the slave of the flame, now coming to life again, lapping its way out of the mud and to the bowl of water I delivered in trembling hands.

III

On the evening of the day I became one of them, I ran into Andy, the eleven-year-old son of the owners of the house next door. I asked him in German what was being erected in his backyard and he told me with a cocked grin that it was a secret. What kind of secret, I wanted to know, but that drew a disapproving look reminiscent of the one the boy's father assumed every time he saw Andy talking to the heathen writer I am.

"Well," I said, "you can at least tell me when it's going to be finished, can't you?"

"*Drei Wochen*," he said, bounding off before I could try to coax anything else from him.

Three weeks. Such a short span when compared to, say, everlasting life. But it was precisely the length of time that Byrd, to my utter disbelief, had told me we had to prepare for Christ's return. Apparently the groundwork had long since been laid, leaving only the logistics associated with the site selected. Which wasn't nearly the task it would have been if all the supporting matter, the signs and the rumors and the precursors, existed in anything less than a global context. I was there merely to fine tune the thing, to correct their mistakes. Indeed, I was more an editor than a scriptwriter, with the exception of the one big decision of location.

~

We settled upon a hill above the Neckar River valley in Baden-Württemberg, a site random, beautiful, and not an hour from my home. At first Byrd refused the stipulation that it be so near to Stuttgart, pointing out, logically so, that if anyone were to ever connect me to the thing, the whole show might be found out. I told him then what I tell you now: With a genetically bred Jesus and two billion potential Lazaruses in the fold, what difference did it make?

And that is what he was, our Christ. A Son of Modern Man tailored to the purpose through generations of breeding and decades of privately funded underground science that would have started wars no matter what its application. That I was a player in its unleashing upon the world at large was, in a way, a fulfillment, a coda if you will, of my own work to unveil the truths of society. Never mind that it was perpetrated by the very liars I had exposed in the past. All advances toward enlightenment were worthwhile.

Which was why I was there, instead of Rome, or the Bible Belt, when the stage was finally erected. I'd had on the news, with its talk of Madonnas in South America and rivers running red in Europe and America alike, when I heard, like the single bell of a carillon, the last nail driven in. I stepped outside, crossing the carefully manicured grass of my palace in the vineyards to an advantageous position among the shrubs, and there he was, the simplest of creatures, ascending the five steps of the impressive platform to his moment of fame. Neighbors had gathered, by some invitation that had doubtless failed to find its way through the pages of my ill-reputed work to me. The Messiah assumed his stage with the air of the ages, hands only slightly quivering as he opened the Book to recite His Word.

> *I've haunted the brink of the murkiest well*
> *Where blow the worst storms, where work the worst spells.*
> *And memories dawdling, yea, memories earned*
> *Like blood-soaked garments into my flesh burned.*
> *Upon twisted roots in the crumbling rock grown*

Whilst 'round me the rattle of leaves like old bones
I've sat and I've mused o'er the spiraling depths
Like Death at its vigil, like Judas undressed...

The next two stanzas had never rung as true to me as the first and so I left the poem for my own thoughts. I tarried there in the bushes till the audience and its entertainment dissipated, till the sun had fallen a last time and the moon risen in crimson; then I approached the stage. Its material felt strange beneath my feet as I ascended to the spot where an innocent boy had stood in all his admirable poise and recited a verse from school. For there was about the stage a solidity that belied its context even as it sought to provide footing where footing was lacking. There was about the stage a permanence that could never exist in the world of men and their schemes. Yes, an Andy had stood here and waxed romantic, and the world, in its turn, had not rejected him. We are creatures of the world, and the world of us, and the tie between us a sliver of a cord.

As I gazed into the surrounding dark, the poem's second stanza filtered back out of the nothingness, an echo returning to its place of origin. A fanciful wind seemed to carry the lyric.

Oh banished all goodness and darkened all days
Though guilt be a dagger like fire through the haze
And vanquished all futures and slaughtered all hope
Though hangs there remorse like a weather-worn rope.
For peace will ne'er visit the murkiest well
As surely as chaos, the rapture of hell
Will scramble in haste from the pulse in the vein
Of one who has been there and bears but the stain.

I drew forth the knife that the Son of Modern Man had left me as a keepsake of our enlightening meeting and held it against the bloody moonlight, knowing the deed I'd been obligated to do since the first tug of the strings.

An hour's journey might have been a moment's in the everlastingness of things. Enough time to remember and dismiss and remember again the third and last stanza in a poem that had no end.

The Horn on Which the Fruit Blossoms

The night before they sheathed me in the suit of Morpheic foam, which marked Ignition Point in the project's progression, all the subliminal images the team had been bombarding me with in the sensory deprivation tube converged into a dream more vivid and intense, more cognitively pure than any I have before or since experienced. The clutter and random deviations that are inherent to dreams were absent; the edges were sharp, the sensory impressions true, the canvas alive. While artificial enhancement might or might not have been at play here, I knew I was getting a taste of what tomorrow would be like.

As chaotic a scene as I encountered upon emergence from the nothingness of deeper sleep, I cannot say it found me suddenly. My first moment of awareness involved looking up from the stream flowing darkly beneath the bridge on which I stood and beholding a battle I already knew raged in the night. The flying white robes and clanging armor, the flashing blades and pounding maces were imbedded in my irises and heart, which ached in equal measure at what occurred around them. What shock was to be had arrived moments later when a mighty black horse from whose brow protruded a single spiraled horn that might have been sculpted out of obsidian burst out of the clamor snarling madly as it gored or beat down all who stood in its path. The comparatively diminutive rider of this blood drenched mockery of that gentle creature of fairytales seemed at first superfluous, an unnecessary prop, but as the tide swept them closer, I realized that she was a woman—which itself bore significance. Still, the axe she wielded somehow never once touched those within the sphere of her strokes. While the sidesteppers of the storm she rode were few, it seemed she intentionally missed short or wide, so as not to steal any of her beast's ecstasy.

The dream peaked when the eyes of rider, then mount, met my own through the turmoil. While her crystal blue irises were of a potency to set the night and all who occupied it ablaze, they could not compete with the silver fire of her steed's, penetrating deeper than flesh, deeper than soul to the very primordial material from which all of it sprang. The realization that I knew both woman and beast as intimately as a stitch knows another stitch in an interwoven work was my last memory of the dream as I clutched the sheets that ensnarled me, trembling at the prospect of the tomorrow that awaited.

~

With eyes only for their work, the crew wiped my naked body down with the chemical prep then turned to their various terminals and control panels to make sure the number pi hadn't crept up somewhere to thwart the process. The clinical detachment was so palpable, it nearly suffocated the drone of Geno, the project head, as he recited to me a mantra that had long since withered my ears:

"Remember, you will not actually be there. No harm can come to you. While our relationship with our world has progressed to the point where we can effectively tap into her memories by manipulating the temporal carousel, what you will experience is in a way a reenactment based on Gregor Bouillon's description of the scenes in his journal accounts. Much of it will be digitally amplified for the reason we discussed—that no detail go unnoticed. Do not dwell on the fact that we have withheld from you the nature of the myth we are examining. (And no, to answer the question that has been on your mind, unicorns are not the subject matter—though the Morpheus Board would certainly be interested in knowing if the horn proves other than a battle adornment, or God forbid, a figment of Bouillon's imagination, in which case our whole project collapses.) But to return to the point, distractions like that would only defeat the purpose of keeping you open and unhindered as you absorb events. As previously stated, the assessing is for us, not you. You are the nerve, the receptor to our processor. Be Bouillon. Let yourself feel what you encounter as he did. The subtleties are what's important. The subtleties. His writings describe the rest."

The one person on the project who did not remain a stranger to me after all the months was Isla—"a Scottish name for a Scottish descendent, though I don't know how they can possibly know such things." She was real like that, unburdened by her discipline in one of the sub-branches of engineering. As with the first time I met her, when she offered me a wedge of the apple she was snacking on during introductions, she was the one among the group, as the suit and final instructions were applied, to show any signs of seeing me as more than an addition to the machinery. While vacuuming the foam from my face and mouth, freeing the channels for breathing and the conveyance of any thoughts I deemed of the moment during this first session, she said into my ear, "I doubt they'll notice if you spare a thought or two for me as you 'absorb events.'"

It was a kiss from her to me, a seeing me off into another world.

SESSION ONE

The scene was one I'd come across, in my Gregor memory, too many times since returning from Jerusalem. Discarded bodies rotting amid swarms of flies and carrion crows. The corpses were sometimes in piles, other times strewn across a stretch of ground outside a village, still other times arranged a certain way, as in a circle or the figure of a cross—or in one instance, among the branches of a stand of evergreens. This time there was no order about the collection, though a monk leaning too heavily on his crooked staff was on hand to attend to the appropriate consecrations.

There was something significantly different about the picture this time, however. Not only was a man of the church present, so were two other figures, neither of which, said my Gregor sense, belonged. My own sense was not lost to me, though it recognized the figures immediately, it bowed to the perspective of the knight and Crusader's grandson whose body and mind I now occupied. The distance, the lack of conflict between the two viewpoints was such that every aspect of the scene was as virginal to me as it was to him, even to the point of forgetfulness—as the account will describe.

Dusk was nearing, so visibility was limited, especially from my vantage on the hillside I'd been descending when the view opened up and my mount grew uncharacteristically restless beneath me—not necessarily in that order. One of the figures was a woman, her shape and manner as she conversed with the monk of such a quality as to be easily identifiable in spite of the fifty or so meters that separated us. The other was a creature I, Gregor, had encountered once before, in the Alps along this same journey back from visiting the city my grandfather and his brethren Crusaders had fought valiantly yet unsuccessfully to win from the Muslims. The one person I met during my trek through the mountains, a shepherd about his flock, had recoiled when I described to him the magnificent single-horned horse I'd witnessed. "The Black Herd," he whispered. "They are spoken of but never seen." When I told him I had heard of a similar beast with a luminous white coat and golden horn, he said they were cut from the same external pattern and nothing more, that to compare them was to compare the fierce mountain wolf to its gentle domesticated cousin. "The White Herd does not mix with the Black, lest their snowy coats end up crimson."

The beast was apparently the woman's mount, though it grazed afield and bore no visible riding apparatus—a rein I would not have been able to see from my distance. The horse was scarcely a silhouette, yet its ebon coat shone in the failing light, as did its spiraled onyx horn. But more brilliant than both were its eyes, twin fiery embers of silver as they looked in my direction, appearing not only to see me and my mount among the shadows of the trees, but to appraise us in a way I found distinctly disturbing.

Nonetheless, it was the woman who won my attention. Her conversation with the monk, heretofore too low to hear, suddenly took a harsh turn as her voice rose in an assault of language stranger to me than the babel they had spoken in Jerusalem. In midspeak she seemed to remember who she addressed, and fragments my ears could understand bled through her obvious rage. "It is your duty…" "…proper burial…" "…sopping fool."

A more careful study of the monk revealed that yes, he was inebriated, and the staff holding him upright was actually a shovel. The incident came to a boil when seconds later he lifted the shovel as if to strike her. Fantôme, my horse, grew more than restless now, snorting and kicking at the earth as though he was other than the veteran of numerous chaotic scenes on the field of battle. I shushed him with an absent whisper, an inarticulate hand, continuing to watch what unfolded below, wondering if I should intervene but knowing it was already too late. The struggle lasted a moment, maybe two, then she was walking away from his slumped body, the shovel slipping from where she had planted it in his face to reside on his lap, a last inglorious rite over this particular scene of Black Death.

"*Lucius*," she called. "Lucius!"

I turned to the field where her mount had been idling, but it was empty. A sudden screech from my own horse, followed by a violent twisting and bucking, revealed why. The beast had stolen up behind us and stood there consuming the both of us in the silver flames of its eyes. One kick and Fantôme was off, but those infernal eyes followed me all the way through the night and eternity beyond.

~

After detailing my experience to the team, from first dramatic impression to last, I could see that Geno, who had nodded a lot during the account, interrupting here and there over particular points, wasn't fully unsatisfied.

"And did you perceive any subtleties in your impressions," the project head said, "that perhaps escaped Bouillon's notice? Were there any discrepancies between the two independent experiences, minus the obvious exception of your knowledge of separate viewpoints?"

"It's a difficult question, Geno, because I don't know that I *can* differentiate. The experience was so surreal, it might have been a dream, indeed was very much like last night's affair. This isn't what you want, I realize, but now that I'm back in the lab, I have to say the most significant reaction I've come away with is how easy it was to be him. Not that the images lose any of their potency. But perspective returns. There, it was all real. Here, well, how do I know Bouillon *wasn't* suffering a hallucination? Or dreaming? Perhaps if I knew what we were looking for…?"

He smiled, a rarity for him. "I will allow you this: We are as interested in the aesthetic as we are the practical, the spiritual as we are the purely sensual. Were you *touched* by anything you witnessed?"

This was a major admission coming from him—and after only the first of three sessions, no less. I sorely wanted to seize the opportunity and ask him to expound, but refrained, focusing instead on what had been provided. It was certainly intriguing, this new aspect to the thing, prompting a swirl of speculation that inevitably centered on archaic notions of good and evil. "Yes. The horse. Its malevolence reeked. Its behavior in last night's dream, assuming those images bear any similarity to reality, could be at least partially attributable to the fury of battle. Not so, its stealing up behind me as if it wanted me to look into those hellish eyes."

"And the woman? Were you impressed by anything about her?"

I thought about it a moment, trying not to let the still active whirlpool of my thoughts interfere. "I sensed in her a dichotomy. The grace of her movements, a certain elegance about her detectable even from my distance, did not match her deed. She could have knocked the monk unconscious, or simply left the scene. She clearly had the advantage over him in his state—no, let me amend that, she would have bested him no matter what his condition. Her reaction, her motion of disarming him and delivering the blow was swift, confident, and, yes, quite elegant. As I think about it, my feelings about seeing her again are as contradictory as she seems to be."

"How so?" said Geno, losing some of his clinical poise to that side of him shared by all men of science, whether they admitted it or not. The side that thrilled in the inquiry.

"I'm not sure I can explain it," I said, catching Isla's equally awakened eye, "other than to say it's to do with the allure all women have for men."

"Yes," Geno said, voice odd, echoic in the palpable silence that seemed to have just then descended. "Yes, I think we are on to something there. Are you ready for the next session? If you want to break for a while to further absorb what you've experienced…"

At the word *absorb*, I shared a secret smile with Isla. "I'm ready."

"Very well. The second scene will likely have even more impact than the first, though not in the same way. Contrary to my previous instruction, this time I encourage you to let your subconscious work on the aesthetic side of it. More will be revealed on your return."

It is all orchestrated by the team psychologists, I thought as they washed me down and reapplied my suit. *The gradual revealing of the subject matter, the false smile, the key words* aesthetic *and* spiritual. I let it all go as the electrons and digits and microprocessors went to work again and the land of Bouillon unfurled before me.

Session Two

When we finally stopped to rest, dawn was only a couple hours away. I bade my weary mount good night but could not sleep because of the images still haunting my mind. For all I knew Fantôme, standing motionless along the rim of the clearing in which we'd made camp, was also still somewhat in shock. But I had seen him like this before, after battle, and the morning usually found him refreshed, even eager to be on the move again.

For my part I could not imagine such a morning. Foes in battle were known things. What we had encountered was something else entirely. Oddly, it was the woman as much as her beast that possessed my thoughts. There had been a sureness about her actions that almost surpassed the stealth and secretiveness of her mount as it whispered up behind us through the trees. While the latter's gaze had been filled with cold amused fury, hers had never left the savage deed of her hand, felling a man of the frock about his pious, albeit temporarily shirked work. There was something terrible in that, something even more terrible than those fiery embers glaring out of the dusk. Her initial intention, one could assume, was of the noble sort, but what concern of hers were the consecrations of the dead? Had one of the corpses belonged to her? If so, she'd given no indication of it. Was she some agent of the Knights Templar riding the countryside looking for those derelict in their monastic duties? I rather thought not.

The small fire I'd built, a comfort in the predawn early summer air, requested more fuel. At first I thought to leave it, not gladdened by the prospect of removing myself from the coziness of the blanket in which I was wrapped to poke about in the dark. Then, as I glanced at the bright scythe of the moon still hanging there beyond the fire's flickering aura, I decided an ample supply of light was available for the task and slipped on my boots. As I passed Fantôme, I saw he was stone at his post, a slow ebb and flow of mist about his nostrils, which didn't turn to acknowledge my presence. I worked the clearing's perimeter to limited success, then entered the trees. Keeping an eye on the fire's glow behind me, I swept the forest floor gathering what fuel I could find, forced to settle mostly on damp evergreen twigs. It was at the furthest point of my search, when I was about to head back with my measly collection, that I heard the soft music of a woman's sobbing filtering through the trees to my right, sending a chill through my body's vessels.

I am a knight of the House of Veianen and it is not my habit to abandon women in distress, but I knew this woman—I knew her not by her voice, but by some preternatural instinct as much to do with her as with me. For the music seemed a call to me, a plea for companionship in the loneliness of her condition, whatever form that took. I stood there for several moments resisting the sorrowful yet somehow beautiful lure of her ululating voice before finally letting my load drop to the ground in surrender.

I found her not twenty meters away in an area where the trees and their canopy grew thinner, the moonlight illuminating the profile of her face where she sat against the trunk of a massive fir, hands on her knees, letting the tears fall. She did not look my way until I was standing beside her, and then slowly, as not to stun me with the brilliance of her icy blue eyes. Meeting that gaze sparked associations that had been suppressed by the spell, causing me to tear my eyes away in search of the lady's steed as I pictured Fantôme frozen back there, frozen and helpless in his own trance.

"Don't fear," said the woman, managing to rein in her sobs. "Lucius is away in the night, by my command. I'm glad you came."

"As though he hasn't stolen up behind—" I quit mid sentence, finding her eyes again. "You're what?"

"I was hoping you would."

"How did you…?"

"I saw you flee. How could I not with your horse screaming so? Lucius meant no harm. He is a curious creature, is all."

I ignored that obvious obfuscation, insisting "But we are better than fifty kilometers from there. I could have been anyone."

"In these hills and their endless forest? You did not sound like a wolf or deer in your clumsy approach." She smiled, a lovely thing in what I now observed was an equally lovely face. Beyond lovely—sublime. And rendered trebly so by the streaks of drying tears.

I willed myself to maintain poise, perspective. For angels did not slay, angels did not ride monstrous steeds the likes of which belonged in the vaults beneath the world, not upon it. Still, I found the extraneous images, even Fantôme's, ebbing from the oval of her countenance, from her words as they softened to the texture of her silky illuminated skin:

"Please sit by me, traveler. Tell me where you have come from, where you are heading."

I did as she bade, telling myself it would only be for a little while. I must trust such softness in a world fraught with plague and bloodshed. Beauty, of all things, rarely lies. Rarely… "I come, lady, from the Holy Land, where my grandfather, Darcy of Veianen fought in the Fifth Crusade. I return to that same beloved Veianen along the Our River, where both he and I were born."

A strange look came over her features as she said, in scarcely above a whisper, "Beloved indeed. But friend,"—her voice returning to its original cadence—"how were you welcomed in Jerusalem, such an unfriendly place for people of the West?"

"Folk tend to be less unfriendly when they are not being warred upon, lady. Do you know Veianen?"

She was silent a long moment, a fresh tear emerging from her eye. "I do. It is there I am going, to defend the castle from a crazed faction of the White Monks, who even now march upon her."

"The Cistercians marching upon Veianen? In God's holy name, why?"

"They have branded it the Devil's Stronghold because the Black Death seems to have left it untouched while savaging all the rest of the region."

I could not find the thoughts, much less the words to refute her woeful message. "But…but would not its amnesty from that horrible fate place it in just the opposite light? Would it not seem a blessed place, to avoid the curse that sweeps the land?"

She looked away, cheek falling beneath a shadow as a cloud passed over the moon, or perhaps her heart. "One would think so, yes," she said. "But God tends to work in contradictions, doesn't He?"

Silence descended like a pall over the senses and the soul, her renewed, subdued weeping, as she continued to hide her eyes from me, only accentuating it. It was I who reclaimed myself first, shattering the fabric with my earnest words. "Lady, who are you?"

She turned to me, wiping her eyes with her sleeve. "I am a traveler like you, returning to my long missed home."

"Veianen? I do not know you."

Her eyes, like that single band of the spectrum trapped in ice. "But you do, don't you? Don't you really? When you laze in a grove remembering nothing but the beauty that surrounds, the tranquility and peacefulness that might have been yours forever, had you but listened to the breeze instead of the wind."

I knew such moments, from far away, in my youth. I knew such moments as I knew her, now leaning to kiss me, to accept me into that oblivion of which our souls simultaneously sang. I forgot my personal Crusade, my threatened home, my chasteness as we were consumed by the moment that might have been.

When it was finished, we fell asleep in each other's arms. The last image to leave me as I drifted away into the landscape beyond oblivion was that of faint twin fires peering out of the retreating shadows of twilight.

~

The picture before me was a desolate and patchwork one: scarred buildings sagging beneath roofs of the color of long dried blood; cats prowling along walls feasting with rats; dusty children navigating a falling pier at which docked a single weathered vessel, its masts as naked as their backs against the hammering sun. I wanted to be a part of this picture, to blend in rather than observe it from a distance. For I knew that it represented all of creation, in its bleakness, its failure, its sense of perpetual digression, the returning to the molten clay of birth.

And yet, weren't those smiles on the faces of the children as they tempted fate by leaping across the chasms between one rotting plank and the next? Weren't those hisses of secret delight issuing from the prowlers as they lost their prey to the holes the buildings seemed to have been constructed of? Weren't those dances of delirium, a delirium that had nothing to do with the heat or the occasional breeze that failed to temper it, on the part of the garments hanging from the windows?

The foreground was rubble, its halls echoing with the scatter of tiny feet as I climbed across the broken stones...*into* the squalid beauty of the picture. I heard from aloft the cry of a gull, another welcome, another accepting me into the deterioration. A song came from somewhere ahead, a song of strings, the stuff of birth viscously swinging across the interim, seeking its lost bundle. My footprints appeared in the ancient dust in advance of my passage, knowing the way home, back to where it all began. The stone trembled in anticipation, the ground rumbled in primal awareness of nature taking its blessed course. The earth quaked, cracked, opened up before me in a gasp of awe to know this miracle again. And when it found its breath, the exhalation brought with it the mounted angel that would escort me there.

Or was the awe to do with me at all? As the angel swept me up onto the mount behind her, I felt the cold that had come up with her, the intent that was at odds with the course. We plunged deep into the picture, driver crying out over the noise of her snarling beast, crying out in furious exaltation to be *loosed* again. Her rapture took the form of words as her finger targeted the skeletal boat in the harbor. In a moment we were there, leaping over the crumbling pier onto the vessel's deck, shattering wood as we descended into the hold, where she swept a rat up off the floor as easily as she had me from my journey home. The rat screeched as she crushed it in her fist, spilling its blood between her angry knuckles, then hurled the limp carcass against the boat's frame.

That quickly, we were off again, the vessel collapsing around us as the beast we rode managed the footing to achieve land again. Its shining onyx horn was our banner as we descended upon the city itself, hoof falls echoing among the walls flanking the narrow streets before finally clacking to a halt at the edge of a square littered with the rickety structures of a produce market scarce few attended. I knew what was coming when she dismounted and approached one of the tables, but had no words to stop her as she rubbed her hands together, then shined the apples, one by one...

~

"My God," I spilled as I woke from the dream into the lab.

"Don't speak," came Geno's equally excited voice. "Let the dream stay with you as we proceed immediately into the next session. We didn't know about the dream. Bouillon's account tells nothing of it. It must have been our influence, *your* influence…"

Words. They had never been enough. Not for this project, whose subject matter would not be concealed however precise their planning, whose potential truth would shake the foundations of science to its porously staunch marrow.

Session Three

I wasn't surprised to find her there at the concealed outcrop that offered the homecomer the most encompassing view of Veianen. The same sense that had told me she'd be gone when I woke from our union also told me I'd see her again, soon. Would that it had been under better circumstances as I cautiously checked the shadows for her beast before dismounting and standing beside her looking down on the ominous fires that encircled the valley. On its central, strategic hillock the fortress loomed proud, majestic, patient against the threat bristling among the surrounding slopes.

"God save this place where I was born," I offered the quietude that spun as from a loom, the loom she was, over the land.

"Where you were born. Where I was born. Where the world was born." The dusk lent her features the same obscure quality as her words as she failed to meet my gaze. "Veianen had a different name then of course…when the continents were one land mass and the evil men do was yet to be done. *God* save this place, you say? Do you speak of the God I once knew?" She raised her hands in an inclusive gesture. "Where is He? Did you see Him in Jerusalem? He is certainly not here."

Still she did not grace me with a glance, as though to do so would be to relinquish Veianen below.

"You are so bitter toward your creator, lady?" I said.

"Bitter? What a soft word to describe my feelings toward Him. Indeed, there is only one I hate more."

Before I could ask for more, Fantôme suddenly jerked against the rein in my fist, blowing in alarm. The lady whirled, hissing into the trees behind us, "*Be gone, Lucius!*" I followed her gaze but could detect nothing in the gloom. As Fantôme's strap gradually relaxed in my hand, I found the lady looking at me finally, eyes mirroring over in a terrible invitation:

"Do you want to see how God saves, Gregor? Follow me and you shall."

~

We slipped noiselessly between the fiery banners, the burning crosses and torches of the White Robes, down into the valley and along the river curving around the castle's perch. As we moved upstream we seemed to gain light and the vegetation a profuse lushness that belied the careful attention the city gardeners devoted to the river's flanks. At first I thought it a trick of the risen moon or the fires from the slopes, or my imagination chasing a pack of wolves across scattered parchment. But as the leaves grew icy sharp edges and the fruits nestled among them an internal brilliance, I knew we were entering her domain, her theater, and I was merely a reflection. When she motioned us to a halt, I knew my penetration into her realm was about to take a different path. Patting Fantôme's muzzle, I watched her proceed to the river's edge, where she disrobed and stepped into the water, leaning down to scoop the illuminated liquid over her breasts and belly. She was home again. Returned from oblivion to this, her birthplace. Mine. Hers. The world's. A world which was in endless recession from her as the beads ran over her skin, the leaves quivered just to be in her company, the apples pulsed with her own heartbeat. So enrapturing was the lady that neither my mount nor myself noticed the passage of Lucius until we saw her beast's tail swirling mockeries at us through the silvery light cast upon the stage. When the horn pierced one of the apples hanging in Lucius's path, the concussion rang indiscriminately through flesh and ghost.

It was then I knew. Then: when the apple was pierced. Still, watching it unfold was like watching a hymnal's pages flutter to that particular offering. The beast turning, transforming into a man; the woman reaching tentatively to accept the fruit from his spiraled onyx penis; the horn suddenly became a serpent, coiling around her arm before seizing the fruit in its great maw and offering it to her very lips; the woman accepting the kiss, and the juice flowing between both their mouths as he mounted her…

And in the midst of it, a third naked figure materializing in response to her impassioned cries, eyes begging through the arc and climax for the fruit that could bring him, too, such pleasure…teeth sinking into the pulp of his granted wish even as the horn punctured his own flesh and the blood poured from him over the eternity they might have spent together, over her belly swelling with the fruit of her garden as she wailed and wailed and wailed until no distinction could be made between her black rhapsody and the savage, pain-wrought chorus of her children.

I closed my eyes in a prayer that implored of its own foundations were they embedded in lies. When I opened them again, the blood was still flowing.

~

I looked up from the image of Fantôme pouring his life's blood into the stream in which he lay to a night illuminated by battle. The flying white robes and clanging armor, the flashing blades and pounding maces were imbedded in my irises and heart, which ached in equal measure at what occurred around them. There was no shock to be had as the mighty black horse from whose brow protruded a single spiraled horn that might have been sculpted out of obsidian burst out of the clamor snarling madly as it gored or beat down all who stood in its path, foe and friend alike. There was no shock as the comparatively diminutive rider of this blood drenched mockery of that gentle creature of fairytales swung an axe that somehow never once touched those within the sphere of her strokes. Nor even when, at the last, she lifted it high above her head, crying, "Not here! Not this place!" and brought it down upon her steed's skull. No, the only shock that came, as its body crashed down upon her, was that I failed to hear the final whisper of her eyes over the tumult.

Still I went to her. I ignored the fighting going on around me and somehow it ignored me, as though my purpose superceded all else. What was that purpose? I didn't know. Maybe just to touch her. To gently raise her lids with my thumbs and look into her eyes again, to imprint forever in my mind whatever ghost remained of their luminous knowledge. To tell her she was a victim of greater forces, that fault lay in heaven and hell, not on earth.

But when I knelt by her, her eyes opened on their own, a brief flash of awareness that included herself, me, and all who had or would tread the world's disenlightened paths back to the womb. It was she, in that instant before her eyes mirrored over in the most terrible invitation of all, who told me.

"Gregor…the one I hate more than God…it is myself. Take the horn back with you. As proof. Proof to the world that it is blameless."

Her lips quivered still, I kissed them and then turned to the beast. The handle of the axe seemed to reach to me, as though the instrument wanted to be extracted, wanted to do its part in dispelling the myth behind the myth. It dislodged from the beast's skull as readily as it had lodged in it. I raised the axe high, deserving this moment, this validation for man and all the evil he wrought. This moment when I hated none above God, including this miscreation before me, darkly raveled into His Design. As I brought the blade down, it was God's goring phallus I was taking, my soul be gladly damned for it.

Alas, the blade missed the bed of the horn and struck the horn itself, deflecting off the accursed thing and ringing louder than the clamor of battle, the noise of my suddenly thundering heart as I watched Lucius rise, tilting his fierce head to bring the point of his horn down to my chest…

~

I'd no words as I woke to the lab again. Neither did the team as they went about reintegrating me with the now. When language did find its way through, it came not in a spoken form but in a written one, its message reflected in the widening, searingly familiar mirrors of Isla's eyes as she sucked the last of the foam from my chest:

YOU WANTED TO KNOW.

Night Watch

1

Dusk had arrived again on Aegea and as usual I dragged Kara with me to the cliffs to see what nightmares were budding among the three spokes of land that comprised civilization as we knew it. The 'Axis,' as our fathers had named the hub formed of Aegea's primary islands, might as easily have referred to survival; madness; the crossroads of man's future and past, surfacing as these fierce bodies of land must have surfaced when they carved their own epoch out of time.

From the outcrop we had an encompassing view of the Axis, delicately illuminated beneath the star-scattered dome. The rising twin moons Isis and Osiris, out of sight behind us, ignited the veins of quartz in the precipitous ends of Roma and Germania, while between the islands the sea tossed uneasily, as if it understood the implications of nightfall. Neither the eye nor mind lingered on the picture's exquisiteness, however, for the first shards of the young night had already made themselves known.

Two vessels carrying flaming pyres approached the inlet below the massive edifice our fathers had erected on Roma's sheer precipices. It wasn't the first time we had stood on the cusp of the virgin night and witnessed this strange homage launched from the island of Germania when the wind was favorable. On the previous occasions, however, the boats had drifted off their original course, as if their phantom helmsmen *wanted* to watch the pyres burn out gracelessly among the rocks below the cliffs, or out on the dark expanse of sea.

It seemed only natural to assume that the Museum, having likely attained an even more profound mystique on Germania than it had on our own island of Britannia, was the object of these launches. On top of the aura surrounding its core function, the structure's Greco-Roman architecture, revealed most prominently in its imposing columned façade, gave it the look of a temple. In a way that's what it was, being the repository for the treasures our fathers had brought with them from ruined Earth when they settled Archipelago.

I squeezed Kara's hand as we watched the vessels enter the inlet. From where we stood we couldn't see beyond the cove's mouth, so we were left to form a mental picture of the flames reflecting on its rocky walls, a ghost dance for the corpses they consumed. We knew that the platforms supported actual human bodies because once, to Kara's dismay, I had brought night vision glasses with us. As usual we mused aloud over the nature of the offerings, which had become, in their way, heralds of the deepening dusk. Were they sacrificial? Had the persons been dead when they were placed on the pyres? They were questions we hadn't discussed the first time we observed the eerie crossing, for we hadn't had the benefit of consistency to help us rule out illusion.

Our voices sounded strange in the gulf, part of a symphony yet to come. That inevitability was hastened by the appearance of a naked man swooping past on wings strapped to his lithe frame, followed by a faint call whose origin was impossible to pinpoint. Not until after its content had dissolved on the salty air, and the figure disappeared around the cliffs to our left, did the word take form in my mind. *Icarus.* I kissed Kara's pale cheek, and she pretended not to wince, knowing it to be merely another ritual gesture welcoming in the long Archipelago night.

Satisfied nothing of alarm disturbed the hour, we turned toward the interior of the island and the roofs of the squat stone dwellings protruding from among wanton tentacles of dark vegetation. I noticed there was more spring to Kara's step now that our home was *in front* of us, making me more aware of my own instinct to seek refuge from the gathering nocturnal forces. She and I were third generation settlers, and the rhythms of faraway Earth were still not unsewn from our physiologies. Any night lasting eleven Earth days would spell a cold, unsettling eternity; on Archipelago, supplement the adjective stygian.

~

Though Kara and I lived as partners (the official distinctions had been forsaken before we were born) and as such were able to combat the night together, being secured indoors presented its own problems, not least idleness. Idleness allowed fear to fester and undoubtedly contributed to at least some of the madness that afflicted the settlement of Aegea. Alas, there was no cure for it as we sipped our hot soup, watching the steam form cousins of the manifestations against which we huddled in our sturdy little abode. If practicality, in the guise of our fathers, had not decided work wasn't feasible during the dusk, then the nightmares would have.

For the dusk was like some subconscious realm spinning hideous images out of the memories and experiences of the sleeper. Only in this case we as a settlement weren't sleeping, and our nightmares were external. To put it in cruder terms, while no proof of sentient life on Archipelago had ever emerged, the planet itself seemed to have the capacity to tap into our memory, at both the racial and personal levels, and to give material form to its impressions. Kara was still not convinced that the pyre-bearing vessels weren't part of someone's recurring dream, even though that conclusion conflicted with what rational theories had been set forth. She knew as well as I did that, rational or not, the theories were flawed because of the very randomness on which they focused.

These were the sort of speculations that filled the idle pockets between sleep. Thankfully the periods of unconsciousness averaged fifty to sixty percent longer during the Archipelago night than they did during the two plus weeks—by Earth measure—of daylight. Our sleeping dreams were infrequent and comparatively tame, as if to provide a sort of psychic equilibrium to our experience of the place we now called home. That Archipelago did not attack our mechanisms made sense only in the logic that a chunk of inanimate matter does not attack. Otherwise, and at all times, we remained poised.

Finishing our soup, we decided that the new dusk provided a sufficient enough excuse to dip into our finite supply of the woody vine we used for fireplace fuel. Since the station on Germania had ceased to function, Britannia drew its power from the backup source of the ship that had landed our fathers here. The rationed *mosel* vine, while technically a luxury, was valued for more than its warmth-giving properties. Its vapors had a narcotic effect, contributing to various aspects of the stand against the night: conversation, mood, sleep. Indeed, more than a few of the inhabitants of Britannia had closed the flues of their chimneys and let the mixture of opiate and carbon monoxide lull them to their easy and anesthetic deaths. Kara and I had ourselves touched on the topic, during the idle hours.

As we relaxed into the atmosphere she asked me if I wanted some wine. We were lucky enough to be situated on the western rim of the island and grew our own grapes—one of the fondest treasures from Earth—on the slope in front of our dwelling. With society, like civilization, existing in the most illusory sense, this seasonal pursuit not only occupied, but also helped to validate the daylight hours. I told her I'd love to have some, and wondered if it would lead where I so hoped it would lead. We had not made love, if such it could be called, since last nightfall.

Before taking the extended glass, I kissed her hand. For a moment I thought I saw life in her eyes, bright as the reflection of the fire in the glass, but it might as easily have been my imagination as she was glad to have the glass out of her hand. Once upon a time she had clung to me, my strength, in her bid against the dusk. Now she seemed to believe it was somehow my fault, that the terrors of the night had been spawned by my own mind. Or perhaps what she despised was my inability, the impotency of all of us in the face of our lot.

"Will you play one of your songs for me?" I asked her.

"Richard, you know the Medievals don't like it." She referred to our closest neighbors, who had a monkish, whimper-prone dog, their own keen sense of hearing, and a dangerous habit of haunting their terrace after nightfall. Their way of dealing with the sense of doom that resided with all of us was to treat everyone as though they carried plague.

"Then play quietly. Don't sing if you prefer. Besides, who cares?" They were old, battered words.

"Would you have that attitude if they sent their monster of a son over here to bash our skulls in?"

My expression, intended or not, spoke for me.

"Is that what you want, Richard?" she said, defiantly.

"I just wanted to hear one of your songs."

She seemed to lose her resistance at those words, though she did not go to the keyboard, dusty like the days at its station along the wall.

"Something has to change," I said, amazed that the utterance came from my own lips. It was my policy, program, and philosophy to avoid at all costs, for my own sake as well as Kara's, any negative language.

She sat on the hearth, sipping her wine, watching the flames. "You have something in mind?"

"Maybe," I said.

I watched a change visit her features. Amid the narcotic fingers of the fire, a forgotten intensity. "What?" she said on a breath.

"A pilgrimage," I said.

"Pilgrimage?"

"To the Museum."

I could tell by the way she turned back to the fire that I had just sapped the last hope out of her.

II

The beginning of the decline of rational thought on Aegea coincided with the departure of the sea ships built by the original settlers. Once used to extract and transport building materials and to lay the cable that had carried power across the ocean floor, the ships had fulfilled their ultimate destiny by going abroad to probe Archipelago's natural resources and explore other island chains, never to be heard from again. Superstition wasn't necessarily born in their wake, but it flourished there…in uncertainty, in loss, in ignorance.

For along with our ships went our engineers and scientists, whom we never in a thousand aeons expected to lose to the climatic utopia that was Archipelago, the hope of humankind. We could not know that as each ship surrendered communications to the curve of the planet we fell back a half century, our ruined Earth in a sense becoming a fact of our future, not our past. The dusk itself became the present: to which one succumbs or from which one awakens.

Yet technology posed only a fraction of society's worries. The isolated nocturnal 'projections' that had merely puzzled the original settlers (most of whom had attributed them to natural causes like the composition of the air and the pollen of the mosel vine) had increased many fold over a generation, giving rise to the idea that our memory had been invaded. The possibility that this invasion had struck our ship's computer banks and the Museum's archives, as opposed to our own mental stores, was considered and dismissed. For the manifestations were at times personal beyond comprehension.

While the phenomena spared neither of the two populated islands, Germania was affected more severely than Britannia, exhibiting signs of outright anarchy—if such a term could be used in an environment where political agenda had become a meaningless concept. *Lunacy* perhaps better applied to Germania's situation as its inhabitants destroyed utilities, communications, and much of its watercraft, disassociating itself entirely from Britannia. The Office of Affairs—for Aegea, for Archipelago, for humanity as a whole—also perished in the process.

Though little better than two kilometers separated the two bodies of land, they might as well have been on opposite sides of the planet. All attempts to access Germania were met with violence: vessels were destroyed, lives taken, pleas ignored. In a relatively short span Britannia's population of nineteen hundred was reduced to sixteen hundred, while the figures for Germania—fifteen hundred initially—remained unknown. Humankind had been divided again, and by the same hackneyed culprit—memory. The instinct to survive, which the species historically was all too good at, now reigned supreme. That it flirted with metaphysical incarnations was to be expected, for this too resided in our genes.

In the face of it all, on the harsh rugged island that hadn't been fit for habitation, stood the Museum. Intended to remind the settlers of the might, will, beauty, and fortitude of the species, it grew instead to represent what humankind *once* had been. The tours to its solemnly attended treasures faded out, rendering Roma as isolated as its companion islands. In the wake of this alienation legend was born, perhaps best exemplified in the tale that the last Germanian boats to carry the curious to Roma had not returned, and this was the reason behind the pyres they launched. But fear was only one component in the Museum's elevation to shrine. It achieved its reverential status by becoming greater than its audience of farmers and netsmen, an enigma to the very engine that sustained its meaning. The treasury/monument transformed into an Ark of the Covenant, only to be known by the initiated.

Of which there were none.

~

Kara knew me well enough to realize that I had been deadly serious about crossing to Roma and the Museum, which was why she didn't speak to me through the next several waking cycles. At first I tried to coax her into conversation, shelling the last of our fresh *cephoids*, unburying one of our older wine bottles, building yet another mosel vine fire; but she merely ate, drank, and inhaled in silence. In bed the sheets remained as crisp as the air, our bodies scarcely touching. I had not seen her so distant since before the last dusk, when we had taken our obligatory turn at the most difficult question facing what was left of humankind—whether or not to have children.

As the night evolved so did its mares, appearing in the most gentle ways at first, then digressing horribly. Doors and windows shielded the brunt of it, but in time the house begged to be aired out. We did this at least once during each dusk, usually after much debate, and more often than not to the end satisfaction of having reacquainted ourselves, if superficially, with the external world. I encouraged Kara to go to our bedroom, but she defied my wishes, stepping out onto the very stoop with me, surrounded by descending temperatures and an infinitude of stars.

Predictably, the Medievals were out on their terrace tempting the night. Their terror-sick hound sniveled more noisily than usual inside the door as our neighbors' monster of a son happened to be walking up the path from the sea, a bloated fishing net tossed over his shoulder. I hadn't realized Egon dipped at night—a risk that only a handful of the more daring or reckless netsmen took— yet I wasn't in the least surprised. When he saw us looking he pointed with a giant digit, doubtless to inform his parents of our emergence. But his parents were too fixed on his approach—behavior emphasized by the dog's increasing whines—to spare us a glance. The reason, while slowly developing, became infinitely apparent.

I had thought I noticed a shadow hugging the slope behind him, but the natural way in which it conformed to the landscape had eased any alarm. Now it stirred, two great wings rising in advance of a long reptilian muzzle, the black pearls of its eyes homing in on the motion in front of it. I shouted a warning at Egon, causing him to stop in his tracks, where he bent his head to look at me as if I were the grail of madness. By some miracle the Medievals managed to pull him out of the spell before the head of the beast descended, brandishing its teeth with a studio-like screech.

I found myself blurting an apology to our neighbors as the lot of us fled into our respective abodes, the sanctity of which the night's terrors seemed loath to challenge. Kara said nothing as we peered through the blinds watching the monster recede. Even if she had been on speaking terms with me, she wouldn't have needed to ask why I felt responsible. The only question was, at what point did this image etch itself into my memory. Its answer did not require searching. The library disc, brought home by my father when I was nine years old, during a time when the appearance of normalcy still had some value, had affected me strongly enough that I remembered the film's intro: *The Smithsonian Series Presents Airborne Dinosaurs*…

But the reprieve was to be brief. After closing the windows that I had parted to create a draft, I returned to the den to find Kara sitting on the cold hearth, watching invisible flames. The place was cool, and now had the scent of the dusk about it: nostalgia, forgotten seasons, yearnings for a lost Earth that we had never known. It was a breeding ground for the sort of specter that visited us next. The dull knock at the door resonated necromancy.

"Kara? Kara *Ann*? Open up. I'm looking for your grandfather."

I tried to meet Kara's eyes but they were frozen on the door.

"Kara, your grandfather seems to have disappeared. Will you open the door?"

"Not *this*, Richard," Kara whispered.

It meant hope to me, my name from her lips at that moment. I knew what had become of her grandfather, killed on the banks of Germania when her father was only ten. This scene must have actually happened, in some form, some sense, some interim between madness and coping.

"Put your hands over your ears," I told her.

She made the effort, but I could tell, as the words from the other side of the door kept coming, that it was a futile exercise.

"What's wrong, Kara Ann? Have you seen him?"

She hadn't seen him, but she had seen remnants of him. She had seen the boat that had carried first him and later his son to the same Germanian fate. She had seen it returning across the Axis with the naked, still freshly stained body of her father, its captain, suspended from the bowsprit, wrists, ankles, and midsection lashed to the spar, ensuring that gravity pulled at the mouth and eyes of his inverted face, staring ahead of the ship like some lunatic experiment in perspective. She had seen her mother grow cold at the sight, never to recover.

"Have you seen him?" repeated her grandmother's voice.

"*Go away!*" I yelled at the door. But it was belated, by many years.

"This can't go on," Kara said to me then.

Which was what I passed on to the gray decrepit woman whom I dared open the door to, in the theater of Kara's whispers. She did not crumble before me, but neither did she knock again as I put my back to the freshly locked door and knelt before Kara, who wept copiously.

There, at the progressing hour, I convinced her. My reasoning was dreadfully simple: we could wait indefinitely to die, or we could go out and attack the dusk, which would never end while it held dominion over our souls. She did not ask what specifically might be gained by visiting the Museum, and I did not have to confess that such was a mystery of the muse which had settled by my ear. She was also gracious enough not to bring up the subject of my parents, who had walked out of their house one night—"holding hands and looking peaceful," according to one neighbor's account—never to be seen or heard from again. These were diversions from the thing itself.

The temple stood there, a harbor of secret truths. In secrets lay possibility, that cousin of hope. In truth lay death, perhaps the next best thing.

III

We dressed warmly and for rugged terrain, in boots and our toughest fibers, with two days' provisions—our answer to an indefinite value—in my backpack. As we stepped out into the night we were nearly overwhelmed by its beauty. The dome exploded with nebulae from somebody's memory of telescopic photographs, colors bleeding into the moons Isis and Osiris without compromising their majesty. As we walked past the Medievals' abode, their faces hovered at the windows, suspicious, incensed, perhaps jealous as they saw that we were not soon coming back. I watched Egon's finger trace the sign of infinity—which had come to symbolize human survival—in condensation. The gesture stirred me; I hadn't thought him capable of such.

Passing our vineyard, already aglow with frost, I wondered if I would ever pluck fruit from its vines again; indeed, whether this were the last time I would experience the view from above the neat rows of mine and Kara's labors. If so, the hour's vision was a fitting one, combining the elements of the spectacular lie that was the sky, the genetically spliced gems that were our grapes, and the mythologically deceptive sea from whose reaches humans never returned.

They devolved into pointless concerns as we continued along the edge of the island till the dwellings thinned out, at which point we veered inland. Moving across the width of the island at an angle, we passed through the fields that grew the hybrid Earth/Archipelago vegetables that withstood the sunless period to feed us at our tables. As I brushed the familiar leafy tops of the plants with my fingers, biogenetic engineering might as well have belonged with alchemy and the lost sciences. The crops ended at the spring-fed stream that served as Britannia's fresh water source and, along with the manmade lake it sustained, provided a habitat for organisms we had brought from Earth. Crossing it, we entered the pastureland that our imported livestock grazed during the daylight hours. This was the most unsettling stretch, for we felt like naked prey without cover to escape to should the need arise. Event spared us, however, as eventually we came to the trail that accessed the island's lower shelf, and the ship that had conveyed our fathers here.

The descending path led us over the severe banks along which three or four netsmen dipped their freshly phosphoresced meshes, which the cephoids were said to swarm to after nightfall. As a strange visual accompaniment, the large fungal plant from which the luminescence was borrowed thrived but a couple meters or so off the water. Occasionally one of the fishermen—as they were still sometimes called—stepped back to extract some of the *ariel*, tossing it out into the water, presumably to help lure in cephoids outside the nets' visual—and, theoretically, chemical—influence.

In another place, another reality, the splash of light on mirror-black water would have been worthy of comment. On Archipelago aesthetically pleasing things, of which there was an abundance, had a way of slowly saturating the soul with disquiet. The spectral sky, reflecting on the metallic surface of the now visible ship, was the perfect example. Though there could be no denying its visual splendor, nor even the resultant internal stirrings, a lover's firmament it was not. For aside from being as ephemeral as the thoughts that conjured the memories, it offered a contrast that was terrible in scope.

In seeming obedience to my own thoughts, a massive Earth-style abode came into view as we crested a rise in the path. Brooding behind sunken shuttered windows and a steep red-brown roof, the three-story construction rested along the shore perhaps halfway between us and the ship. Though I had never encountered its like on Britannia, something about it seemed familiar to me, and more than in its representation of our mother world. Kara had the same feelings.

"Richard, I know this place somehow."

~

As we approached the house we could not determine why it was recognizable to us. I wanted to blame this on some other party, some other party's memory, but the fact of the structure's vague personal familiarity for the both of us seemed to preclude that. It was clearly the dwelling of someone of stature, but its tall, deep dimensions as well as its stern construction distinguished it from some of Earth's manors.

"It has a European look," Kara said.

Which struck me as having nothing and everything to do with the young girl now emerging from the house, waving in apparent distress as she hobbled hurriedly along a narrow walk on naked legs and feet. Her hair shone in the light of the sky, rainbow patterns over gold. She might have been seven, or eight; it was hard to say with so few children around to provide a base of comparison. Kara zeroed on her immediately, sympathy like exposed flesh in the vault of the night.

"Don't do it," I warned as she actually appeared to consider going to the child.

"Something's wrong," Kara said.

"You can't make it right." I didn't need to tell her that the house had never been there before. I'd have thought nothing needed to be said.

"What if she is real, Richard?" As though she hadn't seen a host of similar lies. As though mothers allowed little girls out of doors after nightfall. As though she truly intended…

"Kara!" I reached but missed her arm. The little girl, seeing her coming, picked up her stuttered pace, leg damaged by Mother Earth alone knew what among the pages of history, myth, perception, and any other confusion of memory.

As Kara literally fled down the path toward whatever meaning had presented itself to her in the form of the little girl, I wondered if the nebulae hadn't been splattered across the sky in honor of this very occasion. When she reached the girl Kara didn't lift her up in celluloid salvation, but rather dropped to her knee to examine the girl's injury. The girl's eyes fixed on me as Kara held a hand up to show me the blood.

"Who did this to you?" I heard across space.

When a reply wasn't immediate, Kara directed her attention on the door of the house. As she rose to her feet the motion struck me as terribly resigned, as if she had run through every possibility and had no other choice in the matter. Again, I submitted a warning. Again, they were only words as she strode toward the ornate entrance to domains unknown.

She ignored the knocker, seizing the doorknob in her fist and cast the door wide. As she stood there gazing into blackness the little girl, in a faraway voice, produced a name.

"Lucian."

It was then I knew exactly what house we looked at, and why we should have been moved by it. The residence of Lucian Kovic, ambassador of one Balkan country to another, had been the site of the crimes that had led to the ruin of Earth. In Kovic's house, after he had fled from impending discovery to his own country, the horribly desecrated bodies of twenty-four local children had been found. While the acts themselves constituted an event of global proportions, it was his country's refusal to extradite him that had caused the rift across Europe and the world, leading ultimately to…

A macrocosm of the chaos we faced right here on Archipelago.

"Don't go in there!" I shouted.

Abstractly I noted the loss of the art of the sky—the curtain of dusk seeming to fall a second, hurried time, though Isis and Osiris maintained their posts. Kara, like the little girl behind her, deepened to a silhouette. As I rushed across the yard at an angle to the door, I watched her shadowy hand dissolve before her person into the depths beyond the gaping entrance. By the time I arrived she was inside, and I was suddenly aware of the frost solidifying among the threadbare edges of my adrenaline. The dusk narrowed to the fathomless densities behind a cave mouth. A little girl's hand touched the back of my arm.

I looked into a delicate and sober face. Gone was the rainbow in her hair; the strands of gold were now opaque in the moonlight. "Are you real?" I said.

She touched her lips with a finger, then bid me draw closer. "Is *she* real?" she said in an accent and pointed into the darkness that had swallowed Kara.

I knew as I entered that this might be the end of me, but I had no other choice. For me there was Kara and there was the dusk, a chiaroscuro of infinite shades and angles ending in light or in darkness, or in both. All else, including myself, remained shadow. A lesser philosophy would have failed on penetration, for my cousin phantoms swirled within the place, whispering in Slavic and Greek tongues, haunting its indefinite withins in murmurs and occasional releases of unnamable emotions.

Kara's name off my lips sounded flat and unwelcome in the darkness as some internal mechanism directed me to describe aloud how the end had begun here, in this dark place, where innocent children had been stapled with the banners of war. I spoke of how the idea of children was now shunned, though mankind knew it would die out here on Archipelago without them. The darkness was my confessor as I asked for absolution for my race and species; courting it as it begged to be courted.

Then I heard Kara, with her own aspirations to the religious. *God*, I heard from her. *God oh God.* And I knew she had found the place where Earth had died. I could not imagine looking upon the scene, and prayed that the darkness suffocate me, that its phantoms tear me apart before I was forced to lay my own eyes upon the atrocities left by one racial incarnation. For a moment I thought they answered, but it was Kara descending on me out of the gloom, flailing and screaming.

An ambassador herself: an ambassador of the dusk.

IV

She was silent as we walked around the sleek rim of the ship towards the harbor. At first she had clung to me, but now, conspicuously, no part of our bodies touched—as if *I* had mutilated children. The night had grown oddly calm, lacking any immediate sensory evidence of the ongoing pageant of our memories. I could only hope the lull would hold as the schooner stamped with the faded name *The Viking* came into view among a morose company of lesser vessels.

I glanced beside me but Kara's expression revealed nothing beyond the set-in cold as she gazed in the direction of the boat that had carried her father's defiled corpse beneath its spar when it returned from Germania, otherwise empty. It was necessary to pass over the moorings where *The Viking* was tied off in order to reach the six-meter, two-masted sailing craft that had been built by my family and would convey its lone surviving member to Roma after so long a sabbatical. I thought to ask Kara if she would be okay, but I knew it was an impotent question. She remained unreadable as we passed the ship, which looked not merely weathered, but also haggard from the knowledge of having delivered men, her father and grandfather among them, to their deaths.

Either I had forgotten or hadn't cared to remember how close *The Sprite* was docked to *The Viking*. As I went about raising her sails, Kara stood on the pier looking across a distance of no better than half again the bow-to-stern length of the object of her scrutiny. The temptation to seize her and shake her was great, but the ice around her features had thickened and this was doubtless my one chance to make the crossing to Roma in her company. I worked speedily to obviate any second thoughts on her part, and had I possessed three hands, time might have proved my partner in the matter. Alas, when I glanced up from securing one of the guy lines, she was walking in the direction of the larger vessel.

"Kara, what are you doing?"

"I can still see it," she said without breaking stride. "I can still see the stain."

The stain. I'd heard it spoken of—not by Kara; never by her—the hull washed in the blood of her father's crew, whose heads had apparently been held over the bow as their throats were opened.

The way she spoke the words made me wonder whether her claim referred to the past or the present, though I knew I wasn't going chasing shadows with her under the deck tarp secured outside the bulwark beneath the spar. As I watched her stop before the vessel, perhaps she needed only to confront it, to gaze more closely at its memories, to touch that part of it that had borne her father's weight, been the guide for the poetry his dead body had formed. Maybe then, having traded a greater demon for a lesser one, she would be ready to embark.

Testing the wind with a finger, I looked towards the north. I could not see the Museum beyond the curve of the island, though I was able to make out the distant end of the long body of rock that was Roma, configured fiercely against the moonless half of the sky. The ocean between was slightly troublesome, unlike itself at this hour, even in the powerful gravity of the partner moons. As I watched its tossed surface I willed Kara to make good with her ghosts and let's be on our way. I sensed her gaze when she diverted her eyes my way, in seeming obedience to my wishes. She appeared to smile at me across the water, though it might have been the manifestation of whatever epiphany inspired her to suddenly forsake the ship without even a farewell glance.

As she approached, motion occurred behind her. Against my every conditioning, the tarp peeled away from the bow to reveal a naked tattered figure rising from the vessel's deck and scampering across its ropes to the platform on which Kara walked. I knew the dangers of reaction, of facilitating what could only have been a memory in a nightmare; yet the visual imminence of the event, the wings that seemed to erupt from the shriveled body forced me to open my mouth in a silent warning.

Kara read my urgency if not its cause as she increased her pace, rounding the corner of the pier at a run, reaching across nothingness to grasp my hand. Only at the last, after I'd pulled her into the boat, did she venture a glance back. As I yanked the rope free of its knot and pushed us off, I saw that look surface again: a smile that was not quite a smile as she witnessed her wraith father reel like a flightless bird before the cold water surged up to take him in.

Then we were upon the sea, sails filling with dark wind. For me, the event that had seen us off dissolved into a sense of dislocation, of horrible resignation in the face of impending doom. I resisted it, knowing I must reserve strength for Kara, yet it was she who proved to be the calming force as she finally responded to my touch, kissing my hand and closing her eyes to the rhythm of the waves. At first I was suspicious of her behavior, tempted to categorization, but this conflicted with the music flowing between us, a music that said a found serenity could be a genuine one, whatever the climate, the odds. My suspicion transformed into an unsolidified shape.

I steered *The Sprite* along a parallel path to the bank—to the naked stares of the netsmen—until the Museum came into view, whereupon I turned the wheel toward the precipitous end of Roma, with its temple shining against Isis and Osiris. When, in mid-crossing, Kara opened her eyes to find *The Sprite*'s lone lamp glowing above her, I told her I had put it on so that Germania might observe the daring of which we, too, were capable. I told her it burned in honor of the dead, wherever they had gone; for the sheer faces of Roma looming in quartz and moonlight; for the Museum of our lost Earth perched staunchly upon the cliffs, in defiance of the weathers of the universe.

The waves and wind, intemperate to the naked senses, were strangely accommodating as they delivered us across the Axis, ghosts that we were, to perhaps a consultation with the Maker Himself.

V

By the time we entered the inlet, Kara and I had become companions in the endeavor. She assisted with the sails, the devotion nothing shy of beautiful on her face. As we secured *The Sprite* alongside the boulder that every Aegean knew hid the path up to the Museum, neither of us commented on the twin burned-out husks bobbing along the rocks, unattended, or the skeletons of former launches littering the shore. Nor did we look at the walls of the Museum, a hundred meters above us on some unattainable shelf of the imagination.

The trail was narrow and tricky, indeed perilous. I had read a comparison to the paths of goats and sheep in the mountains of Earth, but the task itself brought the meaning of that analogy home. On an outcrop halfway up, much to Kara's pleasure, I produced a hidden supply of our grape wine. As we sipped the air-chilled liquid our eyes inadvertently wandered up the opposite side of the inlet until they found the place where the walls were no longer natural. In the fashion of an ancient European fortress, the Museum was an extension of the rock that supported it, part of the island itself. That its façade was invisible to us rendered it even less accessible, though in many ways this made the remaining ascent easier.

As we climbed on I did not know Kara. She had gathered a fire into her veins, via the wine or some other, more elusive agent, and become the bipedal form of one of Earth's mountain climbing mammals. When she stood on the lip of the cliffs, breathing through her teeth and hauling me up behind her, this was not the woman that had let *mosel* vine lull her to sleep. She shared my own determination, and the dusk be humbled by the process. The Museum called to the both of us equally; if it accepted only one I would be pleased. I could live with such a ratio, if humankind, ultimately, could not.

While we had arrived at the brink of the pit that formed the inlet, we had still not reached the elevation of the Museum, nor the cusp from which one was said to be able to look back along the length of the almost totally barren island. To my surprise, as we made our steadily ascending way along the rim of the inlet, Kara began to sing. They were little better than whispered lyrics at first, but as I found the notes of her keyboard in my mind, so too did she, letting the music come through her without regard for where we were, our mission, our invasion of this sacred place. Or was it because of such?

I joined in the song with her, though I am no singer, and together we called on Roma to welcome us as friends. With a portion of the inlet's wall still rising above us, the echoes were fabulous; I imagined them reaching the high cliffs of both Germania and Britannia, conjuring new myths in the night. The dusk itself seemed a willing listener as it stretched across infinity, having no better plans now that its nebulous date had gone her way. As I shrank in the vastness of the vault, it struck me that our road had been easy since the harbor, that the dusk was content with memories of memories. If it lasted only until we called at the museum's doors, it would be enough.

The question became that simple as we reached the spot from which we were able to look along the island's length toward its opposite end, where we were surprised to see geometric silhouettes, interspersed with pinpoint lights, dotting the cold landscape. The scattered encampments disturbed us enough that we let our voices die, for we had always been led to believe that Roma, save for the Museum's custodians, was uninhabited. We realized as we gazed on the scene that we might be looking at a lie, but neither of us believed such was the case. The memories were often as elaborate, but rarely as directionless as this tableau.

In any case we knew that the Museum alone would satisfy the mission and so kept it in front of us, leaving the rest of the island to its own affairs. When we reached the wall of the massive structure both Kara and I placed our palms on it, taking in its solidity and reality before opting for the longer route around the building instead of the narrow, precarious ledge along its cliff side. Darkness consumed the path as the structure obscured the moons. We didn't speak as we went, such being the reverence demanded. I thought of the remnants of the vessels below, and I felt I almost understood. Beyond the sheer size of the thing, its presence and power dwarfed me.

Kara's hand in mine was warm. I felt the tranquility she exuded, like something attained through a drug, or a pleasant dream. It was a validation of this pilgrimage, which had no logical purpose aside from reacquainting us with who we were, replenishing the self-awareness that was cyclically stolen from us by the Archipelago night, then returned again, a little less full, by the laboring, reluctant sunrise. In a way it was to the womb we returned. That Kara felt its summon worthy of response made our pilgrimage here the most real thing on the planet, more tangible than its seas, more material than its skies, and yet as broad in its scope as both.

Occasionally we paused to look in opaque windows in the wall, each unsuccessful attempt to penetrate the secrets within rendering the temple that much more mysterious. Soon the corner of the façade came into view, columns and stairs cut against the sprawling view of the Museum's nocturnal empire.

We climbed to the entrance carrying all the hope of our species. At the carved double doors we tried handles that would have been cold even in the daylight hours, stared in windows that stared back at us, pressed a bell that rang only in our own ears, pounded on wood that absorbed rather than imparted impact. No one admitted us, nor was there any hint of anyone within. The building was dark and silent, a tomb: monument of the dead; treasury of their useless and failed pursuits.

I didn't know what I had expected, what miracle might open its wings to us as we returned to the core, but it certainly wasn't this. I turned to Kara with my hands open in apology, but she had seated herself on the utmost step looking out on the vault.

"What are we supposed to do now?" she said. I could see the desolation in the mist of her breath.

I sat beside her, touching her arm to no response. The Axis presented itself below, from this vantage Britannia now seeming as exotic a place as Germania, wielding a similar mythical quality against a sea that had grown angrier since depositing us at Roma's shores. Surrounding Kara and me, the sky was a map of stars, its constellations guiding my eye to the region where I knew Earth to be. I let my gaze linger there, like the echo of her words in my ears. *What are we supposed to do now?* The mantra of mankind.

"I'm pregnant," she said, as if snatching the idea out of the dusk.

"What?" Beyond which feeble reaction I was temporarily dumbstruck. My brain took over, running the numbers back to the previous nightfall, finding they worked out all too well.

"What about the birth control?" I said finally.

"It failed," she said. "Which I hope won't happen with the pill I washed down with our wine earlier."

Pill? But the answer to that was plain enough. She had swallowed an abortion pill.

At last I began to appreciate the nature of the peace that had settled over her since leaving Britannia and its nightmares. It came not from any epiphany, but from the simple decision not to contribute to the survival of humanity. The Museum meant as much to her as it did to me, only in a different, far different context.

The Axis, tonight, looked stygian beyond repair.

VI

There was no other choice but to go seeking a key among Roma's encampments. We negotiated the barren spine of the island in mutual silence, concentrating on the rocky path in front of us as we both recognized the hurt her unassisted decision had caused me. If there had been a philosophical discussion I'm not sure I would have differed with her (after all, suicide had looked attractive to the both of us not so long ago), yet I couldn't help but feel her recent behavior had the makings of more than resolve. It smacked of *surrender*, which had no place in the vocabulary of human beings, however dead they were.

Halfway to the area of population, we began to observe movement around the tents, flashes of color and animation upon an otherwise somber scene. Fires burned low and indistinct—perhaps to conserve fuel, perhaps to remain hidden—their strings of smoke trailing away to the west over the sea and its scattered lesser islands. The occasional torch appeared among the smaller, triangular tents, while the larger pavilions in use possessed stationary light sources. Yet these were mere distractions in relation to the whole, whose increasingly motley denizens preferred the dusk as they moved about in their strange garments.

Kara's voice sounded as baffled, if not as alarmed as I was: "They're in period costumes."

I thought of isles of madness from which ships and crews did not return, of bodies suspended from spars, of fiery sacrificial beacons in the night. "We still have the option of turning back," I offered for dissection.

She smiled at me, as if to say, *You turn back, Richard. We came to Roma for some reason, after all.*

"Stay close then," I told her, like a snippet of dialogue from one of my father's library-discs.

We were perhaps a hundred meters from habitation now, and as that distance narrowed the costumes bloomed into lacy sleeves, and armor, and high collars, and sandals, and constrictive dresses, and flamboyant hats, and boots and swords and parasols and hues without order. Among them were garments like our own, but the greater variety rendered these as peculiar as any of the other outfits. It was as though we had stepped into multiple overlapping eras, their representatives providing the fullest and most visual samples of their respective periods in Earth history. Collectively, they barely gave us a glance as we approached, though the fascination pouring out of Kara must have brandished its own feathers and steel. As for myself, the ideas were forming, but they were as foreign as I was, as we all were in this company.

I took Kara's hand and we merged into their midst without a ripple. Shadows played off of us, as they did everyone else, and there seemed a general gravitation towards certain areas: pavilions, fires, fragments. As we let the force of the night air pull us where it would, a heavily accented voice arrived out of nowhere, alerting me to the somehow overlooked fact that we had all been dancing in silence.

"I know where you two come from," said the reddish man standing there. He seemed to work to express himself. "You come from *here*. From *now*."

I looked at his determined face, the intensity of his dark eyes over his fierce nose, his brazen beard, the frill at the base of his collar. "Are you a memory?" I said.

He touched his forehead, visibly wracked by the strain of the question, then extended his bony hand toward me. "Aren't we all?"

They were only words until they seeped beneath the first layer of my skin, at which point they became prophecy. I abandoned him for Kara, but Kara was not there, having wandered off somewhere outside the radius of my vision, which could not be trusted in any case. I felt the claw of the ruddy man, his beard against my face, the words, "Come, let me show you," in my ear. I looked up into his intense eyes and was a slave to his savage familiarity.

"Where is the woman I was with?"

"Woman," he echoed. He pulled on me until I obeyed, then confided gruffly, "There are such creatures."

I scanned my surroundings for her as he led me between tents to a place on the edge of the dusk, where an easel stood. In its canvas was the picture of a face I knew.

Unable to conjure the exact words, I settled on, "It is you."

He bared his teeth in a strangely skeletal grimace of vanity, or the sardonic, or perhaps amusement, and then waved me away as if I were a simpleton about a thinker's affairs. I went, willingly, his brush carving the strokes of lunacy behind me. Before I had emerged again from the shadows of the tents, Kara was there, in the company of a wizened, simply dressed individual I knew at once to be linked to the Museum.

"I am Pine, the curator," he introduced himself. "I saw you approaching from the direction of the Axis. Welcome to Roma."

~

Disoriented as we were, he made us feel like guests by inviting us into his abode—as he referred to it. The tent was a spacious affair, with twin rectangular effusion lamps in the rear corners coercing subtle patterns out of the multiple rugs that made up the flooring. Classical music played softly from a unit on one side of the shelter, while a woman in ordinary—that is, modern—clothes whom he introduced simply as Abru prepared hot tea on a compact stove. The aroma of orange filled the tent as the curator invited us to sit among swollen pillows along the wall.

Observing our curiosity as we looked around the shelter, Pine explained, "Most of what you see here came from the Museum. We are fortunate to have its generator at our disposal, thus the means to recharge our lamps and other appliances. Roma would indeed be a cold place without. Isn't that so, Abru?"

She nodded sparingly. Looking more closely at her, I saw that she was eastern, probably Turkish, as there were few among us from outside Europe.

"Abru does not say much, like most of Roma's inhabitants." He eyed me with a faintly humorous expression. "Vincent, whom you've met, is as talkative as you'll find here. And I include in that claim the fugitives from Germania—as I think of them—who have adapted over the years to the silence of the others."

I found it interesting, if expected, that the Germanians were the outside element among the costumery. But it was the latter reference I locked in on. "The others. Tell me about the others."

"I suspect you glean much of it," said the curator. "Who among us is not familiar with the styles of Renoir and Rembrandt and Manet? Who does not know the great art of Europe, even in this new unenlightened era in our history? There are conspicuous absences of course, like the pieces that were in private hands, or in America, which of course was already in ruin when Europe became organized in saving its treasures."

We knew the history. Archipelagic man had not fallen so far down the ladder that he had forgotten the expressly human aspects of his exodus. Kara and I knew about how Italy, in the thick of the fighting, had been the first to gather up its great works, followed by France, England, and the rest of Europe; how sacrifices had been made to ensure there was room on the ship, which, though fully equipped for exploration and colonization, had not been designed for this *ultimate* contingency. Every Aegean knew the past. What I did not know—what Kara, as I looked at her, did not know—was how the treasures in question had become so intimately intertwined with the present.

I spoke what I thought was the only possibility: "They are *your* memories, your memories as the Museum's curator."

"You are looking at it psychologically," said Pine. "That has never worked. The memories are in our material, not in a metaphorical psychic well. Archipelago finds her consciousness through our *being*, our *capacity*. She doesn't care, indeed doesn't *know* what our experiences are."

I thought of the theory that sentient beings existed on the planet, though we had never found them. What Pine hinted at was far more incredible. "Are you suggesting that Archipelago, itself, is a consciousness?"

"Is evolving into a consciousness. At this point she has yet to reach the awareness level of the memories that drift outside this tent possessing only the vaguest sense of their identities. Just as they are sketches of what they *were*, Archipelago is a sketch of what she *will be*."

"And what about us?" I said. "What about the human race? What about the death and the madness that have occurred here on Archipelago? What about the ships at sea that never returned? Are we all expendable in the evolutionary path of an inanimate object?"

I felt the weight of both his and Kara's eyes. The curator said, "I suggest the human race knew death and madness before arriving on Archipelago."

"Then there is no hope for humanity?" I demanded. I sensed Kara's eyes shift to him.

"That is not so. Here in Roma, we find that our future lies not *on*, but *with* Archipelago."

Kara's voice was a specter of itself as she said, "No one told us of compromises." When she did not elaborate, the curator looked at me for an explanation.

"She is pregnant," I told him, "and has decided to abort. She took the pill earlier today. You see, this was a sort of pilgrimage for us…"

He nodded his gray head. "You are not the first to have arrived on Roma since the last Germanian boats delivered their passengers here. Nor are you the first to call it a pilgrimage. But young lady, if the pill was taken only today, then you will not yet have passed the embryo…"

"I thought the Museum would be a fitting place."

Pine looked at me again. I had no answer for him, no eloquence for symbolism or irony or whatever it was that sustained her reasoning.

"Then to the Museum shall we go," he said.

~

As we hiked back to the treasury, a much slower trek for the curator's brittle age, clouds moved in over the stars and freezing rain began to fall. We huddled around Pine as he spoke of the coming wonders, particularly those artifacts of the Museum's front hall, which had been selected purely for their *meaning* to humanity.

We had never encountered anything like Michelangelo's *David*, he said, rising four meters tall in its perfect marble representation of man's ability to overcome any obstacle, however great. We had never imagined the suffering exuded from the master's equally magnificent *Pieta*, nor the existential anguish of Edvard Munch's *The Cry*. We had never contemplated such spirit and soul as was inherent in Myron's *The Discus Thrower*, the poetry and imagination of Rodin's—and by association, Dante Alighieri's—*The Gates of Hell*. We had never conceived of the genius, purity, and mystery of Leonardo da Vinci's *Vitruvian Man, Madonna and Child with St Anne and the Young St John*, and *Mona Lisa*.

Or had we in fact known all of those things, even more poignantly than the greatest artist could portray?

By the time we arrived at the treasury's doors, the cold had penetrated through the horizons of possibility to the degenerative tissue. *"Welcome,"* said a pleasant recorded voice as the curator removed his forefinger from the panel inside the door and the lights faded on. One look at the warrior *David* against the backdrop of Rembrandt's living, breathing *Night Watch*, and I knew there were muses to complement music and mathematics. It was their hands, perhaps, that stabilized me as I was lifted up by the artistry and aesthetic power contained within the hall and placed upon the currents of history.

Somewhere between then and the future, I found Kara kneeling by the Madonna and Child, weeping and calling for the love of God to save us all. Before I had completely absorbed the words of the curator as he placed a hand upon her tears, telling her he had quarters in the Museum where the thing could be done with dignity, I heard the embryo screaming. Though it might have been Munch's painting across superficial walls, barren corridors, profound nothingness.

"When you have sufficiently recovered," Pine said, "I will show you, the both of you, a different perspective."

~

She had no name, in a tent with no name. Her hat, which Pine lay over her eyes as the delivery took place, was eighteenth century France, like her stockings, and a smile which only barely knew pain as the child was brought out of her swollen belly into the world of Archipelago. The man who extended his hands to take the wet body from the midwife was dressed less conspicuously than either the mother or her nurse, his garb very much similar to my own.

The curator snipped the umbilical cord, motioning for Kara and me to follow him outside the tent. As we stood in the scented, moist air, listening to the admiration of the father within the shelter, a bird of Earth's predatory variety descended upon us, claws seizing the umbilical cord out of the curator's grasp before it lifted again on its strong wings, angling away across the veil towards the Axis.

.

VII

The rain fell almost continuously as Kara submerged in a sleep so long and deep that I wondered if she would ever awaken. During her retreat into unconsciousness the curator and I spent hours conversing and walking among Roma's strange colonies of coexistence, sprung up like patches of cognizance around the stoop of oblivion. He encouraged us to stay, but I told him we preferred to return to our cozy home and vineyard on Britannia, at least for a while, until we came to terms with what was being asked of our species. Graciously, he refrained from pressing, noting that these things took their own course, with time as an accomplice, not necessarily an ally.

Kara awoke as the first strains of dawn were becoming apparent. As I had known she would when I gave our answer to Pine, she wanted to be on our way without delay. And so we did, fattened or leaned by the knowledge of our pilgrimage, her wonderfully familiar person remaining close to me as we climbed down through the mist that had settled over the island, finding our boat safe and secure by the boulder.

As we emerged from the inlet the fiery vessel approaching from Germania seemed to mimic the ochre of the reluctant sunrise.

A Last Word

I've haunted the brink of the murkiest well
Where blow the worst storms, where work the worst spells
And memories dawdling, yea, memories earned
Like blood-soaked garments into my flesh burned.
Upon twisted roots in the crumbling rock grown
Whilst 'round me the rattle of leaves like old bones
I've sat and I've mused o'er the spiraling depths
Like Death at its vigil, like Judas undressed.

Oh banished all goodness and darkened all days
Though guilt be a dagger like fire through the haze
And vanquished all futures and slaughtered all hope
Though hangs there remorse like a weather-worn rope.
For peace will ne'er visit the murkiest well
As surely as chaos, the engine of hell
Will scramble in haste from the pulse in the vein
Of one who has been there and bears but the stain.

Yea, one such as I, by the road that leads thence
A man as from war, in the profoundest sense
The rages of winter and winter's allies
All traded away for the soldier grown wise.
The wielder within, from the darkness unbound
Beheld in the glass of a sep'rate profound
Which stores all the tears of his penitent heart
For those who have loved him and suffered his art

Yea, those who have suffered his wretched art...

About the Author

Darren Speegle, an American writer, lives in Germany and currently works in the Middle East. When he's not jumping around the world (and often while he is), he's trying to come to terms with all the strangeness through his fiction. He is the author of *Gothic Wine*, *A Dirge for the Temporal*, and the forthcoming *Relics*. Current projects include the novels *The Third Twin* and *Veils*. Find his short fiction in such publications as *Subterranean*, *Postscripts*, and *Crimewave*.

Also by Darren Speegle

A Dirge for the Temporal, Darren Speegle
hc 978-1-933293-38-7, $29.95, 208p
tpb 0-9745031-3-4, $14.95, 208p

Prepare for a decadant feast. *A Dirge for the Temporal*, Darren Speegle's second collection of fiction, bursts with sensations. Like Baroque architecture, plush velvet furnishings or the richest chocolate truffle dessert, Speegle's prose delights all the senses.

This collection heralds the return of the subtly crafted horror tale. A Dirge lingers on the dark mystery of the supernatural, creates the giddy feeling of fear mixed with excitement, that only comes from partial revelations, things half-glimpsed and misty.

Like H.P. Lovecraft or Edgar Allen Poe, Speegle's stories belong to the twilight hour, just after the glorious reds and golds of sunset have slipped away giving warning that total darkness is quickly approaching. Old world legend and gothic sensibilities lurk behind every corner. A world of aching beauty and impending doom awaits. Speegle's work is a rare treat to be savored.

Books from Raw Dog Screaming Press

Isabel Burning, Donna Lynch
hc 978-1-933293-49-3, $29.95, 236p
tpb 978-1-933293-56-1, $15.95, 236p

Isabel's new job as housekeeper at Grace mansion allows her to observe the habits of the enigmatic Dr. Edward Grace. Captivated by his tales of travel to Africa, she is inexorably drawn into a tumultuous relationship which eventually reveals the Grace family's dark heritage and lays bare every secret, even the ones she keeps from herself.

Sin Conductor, John Edward Lawson

tpb 978-1-933293-65-3

Willis Lowery is just your average occupational hazards estimator until one day, while inspecting a factory, he happens across a chemical burn victim. Her name is Dusyanna, and the passion she ignites in him threatens to melt away every fiber of his morals. As he soon learns, there is no escape from her circle of degenerates, so he vows to become the devil to beat the devil.

www.rawdogscreaming.com